W. Johnston

Catalogue of Geographical and Educational Works

Atlases, Maps, Illustrative Diagrams, etc.

W. Johnston

Catalogue of Geographical and Educational Works
Atlases, Maps, Illustrative Diagrams, etc.

ISBN/EAN: 9783742832177

Manufactured in Europe, USA, Canada, Australia, Japa

Cover: Foto ©Andreas Hilbeck / pixelio.de

Manufactured and distributed by brebook publishing software
(www.brebook.com)

W. Johnston

Catalogue of Geographical and Educational Works

W. & A. K. JOHNSTON'S

CATALOGUE

OF

Geographical and Educational Works.

EDINBURGH AND LONDON.

1874.

HAND-BOOKS

TO

Wall Maps of Political Geography.

By KEITH JOHNSTON, LL.D.

UNIFORM IN SIZE WITH THE AUTHOR'S SMALL ATLASES.

This series of Maps is the only one that possesses the advantage of having a special Hand-Book for each Map.

THE advantage of teaching Geography by constant reference to large Wall Maps is now fully appreciated and practised in the higher class of schools throughout the country. In learning by rote from books alone, the eye,—that important auxiliary in the acquisition of all knowledge depending on form—is virtually ignored, and progress in learning is slow and unsatisfactory.

In these Text Books the names selected, and their orthography, are in perfect accordance with those on the Maps. Every place noticed has something peculiar, either in *position, population, commerce, productions,* or *history,* to render it memorable.

Intelligent teachers will here find suggestions which may enable them to lay before their pupils comparative views of great interest regarding different countries and states.

Teaching Lists, carefully prepared by an Inspector of Schools of great experience, accompany each of the Hand-Books. These afford a ready means of testing the attainments of pupils in Map Geography, for acquiring a knowledge of which they offer the easiest method. Every name given in these **Lists** is to be found in the **Wall Maps** to which they refer.

Many practical advantages will be found in this method of limiting the attention of the learner to **one Map,** and its Explanatory **Text Book,** at one time. The distraction consequent on promiscuous book teaching is thus avoided; while, for a few pence, the pupil is supplied with lessons for a great part of the session, and is not under the necessity of carrying to school a bulky volume, of which a small part only can be required.

The Teaching Lists and Explanatory Text are further adapted to be used with **UNLETTERED WALL MAPS,** a series of which, exhibiting the physical features of each country, with the position of the principal towns, but *omitting the names,* has been prepared for the use of TUTORS or SCHOOL EXAMINERS. These are employed either for testing the knowledge of a class by pointing to the **un-named Map** on the Wall, or for filling in the **names** as an exercise for more advanced pupils.

A Hand-Book is given *free* with every Wall Map to which it refers. Extra copies are supplied at the following rates—

Political Geography,	. . . . .	6d. each.
Physical Geography (with Sketch Map),	. . .	1s. ,,
Classical Geography,	. . . .	6d. ,,

LIST

OF

Geographical and Educational Works,

COMPRISING

Atlases, Maps, Illustrative Diagrams, etc.

PUBLISHED BY

W. & A. K. JOHNSTON,

GEOGRAPHERS, ENGRAVERS, AND PRINTERS TO THE QUEEN.

Agents in Scotland for the Ordnance & Geological Survey Publications.

EDINBURGH AND LONDON.

1874

AGENTS
FOR THE SALE OF
W. & A. K. JOHNSTON'S
Geographical & Educational Works.

ENGLAND.

Abingdon	Payne & Son.	Lincoln	Cole, G.
Alnwick	Smith, R.	Liverpool	Webb Hunt & Ridings, and Philip & Son.
Appleby	Whitehead, J.		
Banbury	Stone & Hartley.	Loughborough	Harry Wills
Barnstaple	Marks Bros.	Manchester	Heywood, John.
Bath	Pickering, W. & E.	Marlow	Wickson & Son.
Bedford	Hockliffe, F.	Mansfield	Clarke, T. W.
Birmingham	Midland Educational Co.	Market Harborough	Lawrence, B.
Blandford	Hades, J. T.	Marlborough	Lucy & Co.
Boston	Merton, J.	Newcastle	Bodge, C. J.
Bradford	Brear, T.	Newcastle-on-Tyne	Franklin, W. E.
Brecon	Butcher, Mrs.		
Brighton	Treacher, H. & C.	Newcastle-under-Lyme	Dilworth, D.
Bridgwater	Page, K. T.	Nottingham	Allen & Son.
Bristol	Jefferies & Sons.	Northampton	Dorman, M.
Bury St. Edmunds	Thompson, G.	Norwich	Jarrold & Son.
Carmarthen	Spurrell, W.	Oswestry	Lewis & Owen.
Cambridge	Bowes, T.	Oxford	Parker & Co.
Cardiff	Lewis & Williams.	Penrith	Sweeten, J. A.
Carlisle	Thurnam & Son.	Penzance	Beare & Son.
Chelmsford	Durrell, W.	Peterborough	Hamblin & Co.
Chesterfield	Roberts.	Plymouth	Sollick, J.
Chester	Minshull & Hughes.	Portsmouth	Lewis, H.
Chichester	Knight, R.	Potters	Griffin & Co.
Colchester	Fenton, C. F.	Preston	Cuff, Bros.
Darlington	Bible and Tract Dep'l.	Reading	Golder, J.
Dartmouth	Crawford, B.	Ripon	Johnson & Co.
Derby	Chadwick, J.	Rochdale	Pearse, H.
Devonport	Clarke & Son.	Salisbury	Brown & Co.
Doncaster	White, E.	Scarborough	Theakston, S. W.
Dorchester	Ling, H.	Sheffield	Rodgers, T.
Dover	Harvey & Remmin.	Sleaford	Petty, W. S.
Durham	Andrews & Co.	Shrewsbury	Sandford, J. O.
East Grinstead	Palmer, T.	Southampton	Sharland, W.
Eton Coll., Windsor	Williams, E. T., & Son.	Stafford	Wright, B. & W.
Exeter	Eland, H. S.	Stourbridge	Brownhill, B.
Gloucester	Davies & Son.	Stroud	Clark, John.
Grimsby	Galt, Albert.	Sudbury	Bridgman & Goddard.
Great Malvern	Burghope, T.	Sunderland	Brown, J.
Grantham	Ridge, L.	Swansea	Griffith.
Guildford	Stent, W.	Taunton	Abraham, B.
Halifax	King, F.	Tadford	Groom, F.
Harrowgate	Ackrill, R.	Tavistock	Wright, E.
Hastings	Ospreck, R.	Tiverton	Partheron & S.
Kendal	Wilson, R.	Truro	Heard & Son.
Hereford	Jakeman, E. K.	Wakefield	Allen, B. W.
Hertford	Simson & Groombridge	Wallingford	Payne, R.
Hull	Smith, G.	Warrington	Pearce, R.
Huntingdon	Wood, A.	Warwick	Cooke & Son.
Ipswich	Haddock, J.	Wellingborough	Senders & Co.
Isle of Wight	Wagner, A.	Wellington, Salop.	Lacey, T.
Jersey	Payne, Mrs.	Wellington, Somerset	Unley, J.
Kendal	Wilson, T.	Weymouth	Preddick, L.
Kidderminster	Mark, T.	Winchester	Wells, J.
Lancaster	Milner, E. & J.	Wisbech	Gardner & Co.
Leeds	Bean & Son.	Wolverhampton	Cope, T.
Leander	Vice, J.	Workington	Brannan, H. P.
Leamington	Wippell, H.	Worcester	Williams, W. H.
Leominster	Partridge, S.	York	Sampson, J.
Lichfield	Lomax, T. O.		

SCOTLAND.

J. Menzies & Co.
J. Lumsden & Son, J. Smith & Son, Glasgow.
Lewis Smith, ... Aberdeen.

IRELAND.

M'Glashan and Gill, Sullivan Bros. Dublin.
Marcus Ward & Co. . . . . Belfast.

THE COLONIES.

Geo. Robertson, Melbourne. B. Nickol, Sydney. G. Slater & Co. Brisbane. J. C. Juta,
Cape Town. Thacker & Spink, Calcutta. Thacker, Vining, & Co. and Shivers, Bombay,
& Co., Bombay. Dawson Bros., Montreal, and F. E. Grafton, Montreal.

All Communications to be Addressed—

Messrs. W. & A. K. JOHNSTON,

4 ST. ANDREW SQUARE,

E D I N B U R G H.

OR,

Messrs. W. & A. K. JOHNSTON,

18 PATERNOSTER ROW,

L O N D O N, E.C.

CONTENTS.

Note. — For the present condition of the Ordnance and Geological Surveys of Scotland, see separate Catalogue.

Geographical and Educational Works.

THE
NATIONAL SCHOOL BOARD SERIES
LARGE WALL MAPS AND ILLUSTRATIONS.
By KEITH JOHNSTON, LL.D., F.R.G.S., &c., &c.
GEOGRAPHER TO THE QUEEN FOR SCOTLAND.

This well-known Series possesses the following advantages:—
From the great demand, they are constantly at press, and no Map is ever printed without being thoroughly revised. The Maps are printed by Steam, in permanent Oil Colours. The Series is the most extensive published, consisting of upwards of 60 Maps and Illustrations, to which additions are constantly being made. They are Mounted on Cloth and Rollers, Plain or Varnished, the best materials only being used. The whole Series is of one uniform size, history, 50 by 42 inches. It is the cheapest ever published, the same being Rollers varnished, 12s. It is the only Series accompanied by Hand Books written expressly for each Map or Illustration. These are given gratis to purchasers. It will be found Indispensable to Teachers and Managers who require the Government Grant.
For List of Illustrations see Page 10.

POLITICAL GEOGRAPHY.

Name of Map.	Size in Inches	Mounting	Selling Price.
EASTERN HEMISPHERE,	50 by 42	Roller Varnished.	£0 12 0
	" "	Plain.	0 10 0
WESTERN HEMISPHERE,	50 by 42	Roller Varnished.	0 12 0
	" "	Plain.	0 10 0
ENGLAND, . . .	50 by 42	Roller Varnished.	0 12 0
	" "	Plain.	0 10 0
SCOTLAND, . . .	50 by 42	Roller Varnished.	0 12 0
	" "	Plain.	0 10 0
IRELAND, . . .	50 by 42	Roller Varnished.	0 12 0
	" "	Plain.	0 10 0
EUROPE, . . .	50 by 42	Roller Varnished.	0 12 0
	" "	Plain.	0 10 0
ASIA, . . .	50 by 42	Roller Varnished.	0 12 0
	" "	Plain.	0 10 0
AFRICA, . . .	50 by 42	Roller Varnished.	0 12 0
	" "	Plain.	0 10 0
AMERICA, . . .	50 by 42	Roller Varnished.	0 12 0
	" "	Plain.	0 10 0
CANAAN and PALESTINE,	50 by 42	Roller Varnished.	0 12 0
	" "	Plain.	0 10 0
BRITISH ISLES, " .	50 by 42	Roller Varnished.	0 12 0
	" "	Plain.	0 10 0
FRANCE, " . .	50 by 42	Roller Varnished.	0 12 0
	" "	Plain.	0 10 0
SPAIN, . . .	50 by 42	Roller Varnished.	0 12 0
	" "	Plain.	0 10 0
ITALY, . . .	50 by 42	Roller Varnished.	0 12 0
	" "	Plain.	0 10 0
CENTRAL EUROPE,	50 by 42	Roller Varnished.	0 12 0
	" "	Plain.	0 10 0
INDIA, . " .	50 by 42	Roller Varnished.	0 12 0
	" "	Plain.	0 10 0
NORTH AMERICA, .	50 by 42	Roller Varnished.	0 12 0
	" "	Plain.	0 10 0
UNITED STATES, .	50 by 42	Roller Varnished.	0 12 0
	" "	Plain.	0 10 0
SOUTH AMERICA, .	50 by 42	Roller Varnished.	0 12 0
	" "	Plain.	0 10 0
CANADA, NOVA SCOTIA, ETC.	50 by 42	Roller Varnished.	0 12 0

Name of Map.	Size in Inches.	Mounting.	Selling Price.
AUSTRALIA, . . .	50 by 42	Roller Varnished.	£0 12 0
	" "	" Plain.	0 10 0
NEW ZEALAND, . .	50 by 42	Roller Varnished.	0 12 0
	" "	" Plain.	0 10 0
PACIFIC OCEAN, . .	50 by 42	Roller Varnished.	0 12 0
	" "	" Plain.	0 10 0
WORLD, Mercator's Projection,* . . .	50 by 42	Roller Varnished.	0 12 0
	" "	" Plain.	0 10 0
EASTERN and WESTERN HEMISPHERES (One Map), ...	50 by 42	Roller Varnished.	0 12 0
	" "	" Plain.	0 10 0
TRAVELS OF ST. PAUL,	50 by 42	Roller Varnished.	0 12 0
" " "	" "	" Plain.	0 10 0

* Coloured to show all the Colonies of Great Britain at one view.

CLASSICAL GEOGRAPHY.

Name of Map.	Size in Inches.	Mounting.	Selling Price.
ORBIS VETERIBUS NOTUS, . . .	50 by 42	Roller Varnished.	£0 12 0
	" "	" Plain.	0 10 0
ITALIA ANTIQUA, " .	50 by 42	Roller Varnished.	0 12 0
	" "	" Plain.	0 10 0
GRÆCIA ANTIQUA, .	50 by 42	Roller Varnished.	0 12 0
	" "	" Plain.	0 10 0
ASIA MINOR, . . .	50 by 42	Roller Varnished.	0 12 0
	" "	" Plain.	0 10 0
ORBIS ROMANUS, . .	50 by 42	Roller Varnished.	0 12 0
	" "	" Plain.	0 10 0
OUTLINE MAP OF COUNTRIES Bordering on Mediterranean, . .	50 by 42	Roller Varnished.	0 12 0
" " "	" "	" Plain.	0 10 0

PHYSICAL GEOGRAPHY.

Name of Map.	Size in Inches.	Mounting.	Selling Price.
WORLD, in Hemispheres,	50 by 42	Roller Varnished.	£0 12 0
	" "	" Plain.	0 10 0
EUROPE, . . .	50 by 42	Roller Varnished.	0 12 0
	" "	" Plain.	0 10 0
ASIA, . . .	50 by 42	Roller Varnished.	0 12 0
	" "	" Plain.	0 10 0
AFRICA, . . .	50 by 42	Roller Varnished.	0 12 0
	" "	" Plain.	0 10 0
AMERICA, . . .	50 by 42	Roller Varnished.	0 12 0
" . . .	" "	" Plain.	0 10 0

For Physical Chart of the World on Mercator's Projection, see page 29.

OUTLINE MAPS.

Uniform with the Maps of Political Geography, showing the Outlines,
Rivers, Mountains, Towns, and Political Divisions, without Names.

WORLD, Mercator.	AMERICA.	CLASSICAL MAP OF
WORLD, in Hemi-	BRITISH ISLES.	COUNTRIES BOR-
spheres.	ENGLAND.	DERING ON THE
EUROPE.	SCOTLAND.	MEDITERRAN-
ASIA.	IRELAND.	EAN.
AFRICA.	INDIA.	

FULL COLOURED.

Size, 60 by 42 Inches.

Price, on Rollers, Varnished,	.	12s.
,, ,, Plain, .	.	10s.

SERIES OF

EDUCATIONAL HAND-BOOKS,

TO ACCOMPANY THE LARGE AND SMALL WALL MAPS.

With each of the Maps,—POLITICAL, CLASSICAL, PHYSICAL,
or OUTLINE,—is given a Descriptive Hand-Book, free of
charge. Additional Copies can be had at the following
prices :—

	Each.
POLITICAL GEOGRAPHY, ...	6d.
CLASSICAL GEOGRAPHY, ...	6d.
PHYSICAL GEOGRAPHY, with Sketch Map, .	1s. 6d.
,, ,, with Analytical Index, Cloth,	3s. 6d.
THE SURFACE ZONES OF THE GLOBE, with Six Coloured	
Views and Two Maps, Cloth, . .	3s. 6d.
OUTLINE GEOGRAPHY, . . .	6d.
Hand-Book to GEOLOGICAL MAP OF BRITISH ISLANDS (GEIKIE's),	2s.
,, METRIC SYSTEM, . .	6d.
,, CHRONOLOGY AND ANCIENT HISTORY,	6d.
GLOSSARY OF GEOGRAPHICAL TERMS, . .	6d.
NATURAL PHILOSOPHY (see pages 10-15), Nos. 1, 2, 3, 4, 5, 6, 7, 8,	
9, 10, 11, 12, 13, 14, 15, ...	6d.

JOHNSTON'S NATIONAL SCHOOL BOARD SERIES OF
ILLUSTRATIONS OF NATURAL PHILOSOPHY.

These Illustrations of Natural Philosophy are carefully drawn and coloured after nature, and the series in preparation will include all the most interesting Phenomena of general Science. Each Sheet is accompanied by a Hand-book explanatory of the subject.

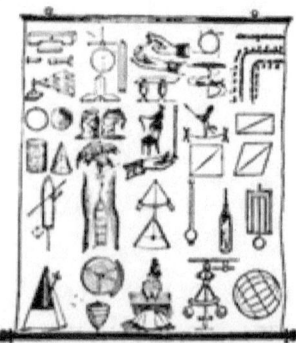

No. I.—Properties of Bodies, 37 Diagrams, and Descriptive Book,
50 by 42 inches, Coloured and Mounted on Cloth and Rollers, 10s. ; Varnished, 12s.

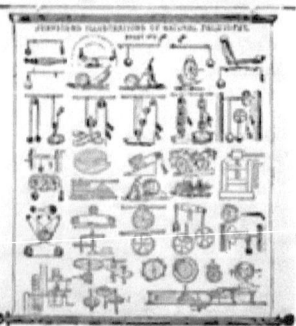

No. II.—Mechanical Powers, 47 Diagrams, and Descriptive Book,
50 by 42 inches, Coloured and Mounted on Cloth and Rollers, 10s. ; Varnished, 12s.

JOHNSTON'S ILLUSTRATIONS OF NATURAL PHILOSOPHY
—continued.

No. III.—**Hydrostatics** 23 Diagrams, and Descriptive Book,
50 by 42 Inches, Coloured and mounted on Cloth and Rollers, 10s. ; Varnished, 12s.

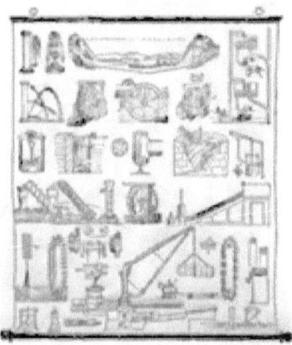

No. IV.—**Hydraulics**, 27 Diagrams, and Descriptive Book,
50 by 42 Inches, Coloured and Mounted on Cloth and Rollers, 10s. ; Varnished, 12s.

JOHNSTON'S ILLUSTRATIONS OF NATURAL PHILOSOPHY
—*continued.*

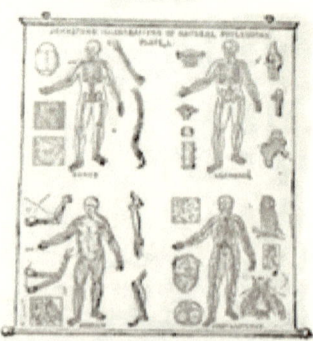

No. V.—**Human Anatomy and Physiology**, Plate 1, 27 Diagrams, and Descriptive Book.
50 by 42 inches, Coloured and Mounted on Cloth and Rollers, 10s. ; Varnished, 12s.

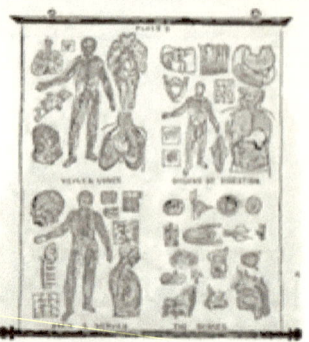

No. VI.—**Human Anatomy and Physiology**, Plate 2, 42 Diagrams, and Descriptive Book.
50 by 42 inches, Coloured and Mounted on Cloth and Rollers, 10s. ; Varnished, 12s.

JOHNSTON'S ILLUSTRATIONS OF NATURAL PHILOSOPHY
—continued.

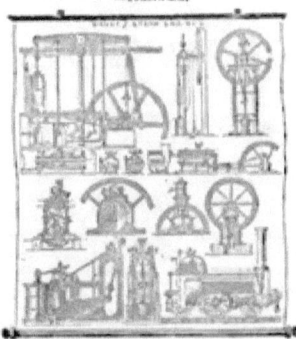

No. VII.—Modern Varieties of the **Steam** Engine and **Boilers,** 15 Diagrams, and Descriptive Book.
50 by 42 inches, Coloured and Mounted on Cloth and Roller, 10s.; Varnished, 12s.

ILLUSTRATIONS OF BOTANY,
BY JOHN HUTTON BALFOUR, M.D.,
F.R.S. F.L.S. SEC. R.S.E.
PROFESSOR OF BOTANY, EDINBURGH.

Sheet No. 1. Organs of Plants, Tissues, Root, Stem, 36 Illustrations. With Hand-Book.

Sheet No. 2. Leaves and their Modifications. 30 Illustrations. With Hand-Book.

Sheet No. 3. Inflorescence, Whorls of the Flower. 36 Illustrations. With Hand-Book.

Sheet No. 4. Pistil, Ovule, Fruit, Seed, Organs of Flowerless Plants. 44 Illustrations. With Hand-Book.

The above were all drawn under the direction of Professor Balfour, and are printed in permanent Oil Colours.

Size 50 by 42 inches. **Coloured and Mounted on Cloth and Roller, 10s.** Varnished 12s. each.

ILLUSTRATIONS OF ASTRONOMY,
BY THE REV. JAMES GALL.

Sheet No. 1. The Solar System.

Sheet No. 2. Astronomical Diagrams.

Sheet No. 3. Celestial objects.

Sheet No. 4. Map of the Heavens.

50 by 42 Inches. Coloured and Mounted on Cloth and Rollers, 10s.; Varnished 12s. each, with Hand-Book.

DIAGRAM No. 1.

SET OF MAPS IN CASE.

The CASE for hanging on a Wall contains 10 Coloured Maps or Illustrations on Cloth and Rollers, and so constructed that any Map can be drawn down as required, and pulled up again by cords at the side.

The Maps measure 4 feet 2 inches by 3 feet 6 inches. The Case is 4 feet 8 inches long by 1 foot 9 inches high; and as it is only 4 inches thick, it projects very little from the wall. It can be packed in matting, and sent with safety to any part of the country.

						£	s.	d.
Case containing ten Maps or Illustrations,		·	·	·	£8	10	0
,,	nine	,,	·	·	·	7	17	6
,,	eight	,,	·	·	·	7	7	0
,,	seven	,,	·	·	·	6	12	6
,,	six	,,	·	·	·	6	0	0
,,	five	,,	·	·	·	5	5	0

. As all the School-room Maps and Illustrations are of uniform size, the Case may contain any of those selected by a purchaser.

DIAGRAM No. 2

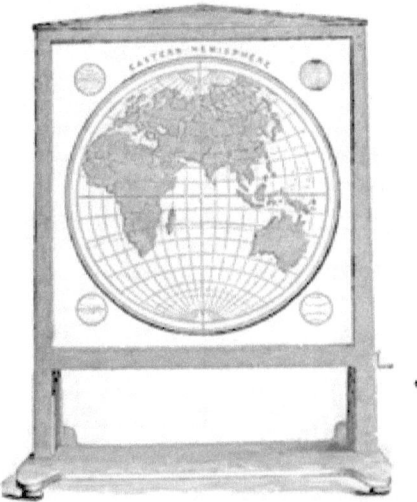

SET OF MAPS IN STAND.

The STAND is mounted on Castors, and contains 16 Coloured Maps, varnished, on a continuous web of cloth, which revolves vertically, over Rollers, by turning the handle at the side, so that the Maps are exhibited in rotation.

As all the School-Room Maps and Illustrations are of uniform size, the Stand may contain any of those selected by a purchaser.

The Maps measure 4 feet 2 inches by 3 feet 6 inches.   The Stand is 6 feet 6 inches high by 4 feet 7 inches broad.   It can be taken to pieces, packed in matting, and sent with safety to any part of the country.   Price, £8, 10s. 6d.

When made with Black Board behind for Arithmetic or Diagrams,
10s. 6d. extra.

SMALL WALL MAPS,

FULL COLOURED.

Name of Map.	Size in Inches	Mounting.	Selling Price.
EASTERN HEMISPHERE,	33 by 27	Roller Varnished.	£0 6 0
		Plain.	0 5 0
WESTERN HEMISPHERE.	33 by 27	Roller Varnished.	0 6 0
		Plain.	0 5 0
ENGLAND,	33 by 27	Roller Varnished.	0 6 0
		Plain.	0 5 0
SCOTLAND,	33 by 27	Roller Varnished.	0 6 0
		Plain.	0 5 0
IRELAND,	33 by 27	Roller Varnished.	0 6 0
		Plain.	0 5 0
EUROPE,	33 by 27	Roller Varnished.	0 6 0
		Plain.	0 5 0
ASIA,	33 by 27	Roller Varnished.	0 6 0
		Plain.	0 5 0
AFRICA,	33 by 27	Roller Varnished.	0 6 0
		Plain.	0 5 0
AMERICA,	33 by 27	Roller Varnished.	0 6 0
		Plain.	0 5 0
CANAAN and PALESTINE,	33 by 27	Roller Varnished.	0 6 0
		Plain.	0 5 0
BRITISH ISLES, "	33 by 27	Roller Varnished.	0 6 0
		Plain.	0 5 0
WORLD, MERCATOR'S PROJECTION,	33 by 27	Roller Varnished.	0 6 0
	"	Plain.	0 5 0
EASTERN AND WESTERN HEMISPHERES (ONE MAP),	33 by 27	Roller Varnished.	0 6 0
	"	Plain.	0 5 0
CANADA, UNITED STATES, AND MEXICO,	33 by 27	Roller Varnished.	0 6 0
	"	Plain.	0 5 0
A Map illustrative of Geographical Terms, with Glossary.	33 by 27	Roller Varnished.	0 6 0
	"	Plain.	0 5 0
CHRONOLOGICAL CHART OF ANCIENT HISTORY, with Glossary,	33 by 27	Roller Varnished.	0 6 0
	"	Plain.	0 5 0
CHART OF THE METRIC SYSTEM OF WEIGHTS AND MEASURES,	33 by 27	Roller Varnished.	0 6 0
	"	Plain.	0 5 0

A Hand-Book is given *free* with every Wall Map to which it refers.
Extra copies 6d. each.

DIAGRAM No. 3.

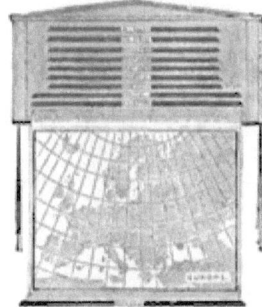

A CASE for hanging on a wall, containing 10 Coloured Maps on Cloth and Rollers, so constructed that any Map can be drawn down as required, and pulled up again by the cord at the side.

———

Size of the Maps 53 by 27 inches.

Size of the Case 3 feet 3 inches by 1 foot 6 inches.

Price, in Painted Case, £4, 14s. 6d.

DIAGRAM No. 4.

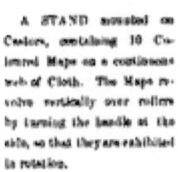

A STAND mounted on Castors, containing 10 Coloured Maps on a continuous web of Cloth. The Maps revolve vertically over rollers by turning the handle at the side, so that they are exhibited in rotation.

———

Size of the Maps 53 by 27 inches.

Size of the Stand 6 feet high by 3 feet 2 inches broad.

Price of Maps and Painted Stand, with Black Diagram Board, £5, 5s.

Ditto, Solid Oak, do., £7, 7s.

ATLAS

OF

THE COUNTIES OF SCOTLAND.

WITH MEMOIR OF SCOTTISH GEOGRAPHY,
INDEX, ETC.

Half-Bound, Price £7, 7s.

*EACH COUNTY MAP MAY BE HAD SEPARATELY, AT THE
FOLLOWING PRICES:—*

One Sheet.

	In Sheets.	Case.	Roller Varnished.
BERWICK,	5s.	8s. 6d.	10s. 6d.
BUTE,	5s.	8s. 6d.	10s. 6d.
CAITHNESS,	5s.	8s. 6d.	10s. 6d.
DUMBARTON,	5s.	8s. 6d.	10s. 6d.
HADDINGTON,	5s.	8s. 6d.	10s. 6d.
KINCARDINE,	5s.	8s. 6d.	10s. 6d.
LINLITHGOW,	5s.	8s. 6d.	10s. 6d.
MORAY AND NAIRN,	5s.	8s. 6d.	10s. 6d.
ORKNEY,	5s.	8s. 6d.	10s. 6d.
PEEBLES,	5s.	8s. 6d.	10s. 6d.
RENFREW,	5s.	8s. 6d.	10s. 6d.
SELKIRK,	5s.	8s. 6d.	10s. 6d.
SHETLAND,	5s.	8s. 6d.	10s. 6d.
SKYE ISLAND,	5s.	8s. 6d.	10s. 6d.
STIRLING,	5s.	8s. 6d.	10s. 6d.
SUTHERLAND,	5s.	8s. 6d.	10s. 6d.
WIGTOWN,	5s.	8s. 6d.	10s. 6d.

Two Sheets.

	In Sheets.	Case.	Roller Varnished.
ANGUS,	10s.	15s.	18s. 6d.
ARGYLL,	10s.	15s.	18s. 6d.
FIFE & KINROSS,	10s.	15s.	18s. 6d.
KIRKCUDBRIGHT,	10s.	15s.	18s. 6d.
LANARK,	10s.	15s.	18s. 6d.
ROSS AND CROMARTY,	10s.	15s.	18s. 6d.
ROXBURGH,	10s.	15s.	18s. 6d.

Three Sheets.

	In Sheets.	Case.	Roller Varnished.
WESTERN ISLANDS,	15s.	25s.	31s. 6d.

Four Sheets.

	In Sheets.	Case.	Roller Varnished.
ABERDEEN,	20s.	30s.	35s. 6d.
AYR,	20s.	30s.	35s. 6d.
DUMFRIES,	20s.	30s.	35s. 6d.
EDINBURGHSHIRE,	20s.	30s.	35s. 6d.
INVERNESS,	20s.	30s.	35s. 6d.
PERTH & CLACKMANNAN,	20s.	30s.	35s. 6d.

Plate of the Comparative Height of Scottish Mountains, 5s.
View of the Comparative Length of the Rivers, coloured, 5s.

AN ATLAS

OF

HUMAN ANATOMY AND PHYSIOLOGY.

BY

WILLIAM TURNER, M.B., M.R.C.S. Eng.

Professor of Anatomy in the University of Edinburgh.

SELECTED AND ARRANGED UNDER THE SUPERINTENDENCE OF

JOHN GOODSIR, F.B.SS.L. & E.

Size of Sheet, 26 inches by 21 inches (folded).
Price, with Hand-book, fully explaining the Plates, bound in Cloth, 25s.

These Illustrations have been drawn with great care; they are beautifully engraved and printed in colours, and in the selection and description of the Illustrations, their adaptation for popular use in the school or family has been especially considered.

CONTENTS.

Plate I.—The Bones.

FIG. 1. FRONT VIEW OF THE ADULT SKELETON.
2. SIDE VIEW OF THE SPINAL COLUMN.
3. MODE OF UNION OF THE BONES OF THE HEAD.
4. SECTION OF THIGH BONE.
5. LONGITUDINAL SECTION OF BONE, MAGNIFIED.
6. TRANSVERSE SECTION OF BONE, MAGNIFIED.

Plate II.—The Ligaments.

FIG. 1. FRONT VIEW OF ADULT SKELETON WITH LIGAMENTS.
2. FIBROUS TISSUE OF LIGAMENTS, MAGNIFIED.
3. VERTICAL SECTION OF HIP JOINT.
4. ELBOW JOINT, CUT OPEN TO DISPLAY THE INTERIOR.
5. RING-LIKE LIGAMENT OF THE RADIUS.
6. FIRST VERTEBRA.
7. SECOND VERTEBRA.
8. DISC OF INTERVERTEBRAL SUBSTANCE.
9. THREE OF THE VERTEBRÆ, WITH DISCS.

Plate III.—The Muscles.

FIG. 1. FRONT VIEW OF ADULT, SHOWING THE MUSCLES.
2. STRAIGHT MUSCLE OF THE THIGH.
3. MAGNIFIED VIEW OF MUSCULAR FIBRE.
4. BICEPS MUSCLE OF THE ARM.
5. EXTENSOR MUSCLE OF THE FORE ARM.
6. MUSCLES OF THE CALF.

B

Plate IV.—The Heart and Arteries.

Fig. 1. GENERAL VIEW OF THE ARTERIES OF THE BODY.
2. CAVITY OF THE CHEST, WITH HEART.
3. LONGITUDINAL SECTION OF THE HEART.
4. TRANSVERSE SECTION OF THE HEART.
5. FIBROUS TISSUE OF ARTERIAL TUBE, MAGNIFIED.
6. ARRANGEMENT OF THE CAPILLARIES.
7. GLOBULES OF THE HUMAN BLOOD, MAGNIFIED.

Plate V.—Veins and Organs of Respiration.

Fig. 1. GENERAL VIEW OF THE VENOUS SYSTEM.
2. VALVES OF THE VEINS.
3. THE HEART, LUNGS, ETC.
4. TRACHEA AND BRONCHIAL TUBE.
5. MICROSCOPIC VIEW OF THE TISSUE OF THE LUNGS.
6. CILIATED EPITHELIUM.
7. DIAGRAM OF THE CIRCULATION.

Plate VI.—Lymphatics, and Organs of Digestion.

Fig. 1. GENERAL VIEW OF DIGESTIVE TRACT.
2. GENERAL VIEW OF THE TEETH.
3. SECTION OF A TOOTH, WITH ITS VESSELS AND NERVE.
4. STOMACH, DUODENUM, PANCREAS, SPLEEN.
5. MAGNIFIED VIEW OF INNER SURFACE OF STOMACH.
6. CELLS OF THE GASTRIC GLANDS.
7. GLANDS AND VILLI OF INTESTINE.
8. LIVER, WITH ITS VESSELS AND GALL-BLADDER.
9. SECRETING CELLS OF THE LIVER.
10. GENERAL VIEW OF LYMPHATICS.

Plate VII.—The Brain and Nerves.

Fig. 1. GENERAL VIEW OF THE NERVOUS SYSTEM.
2. NERVE TISSUE MAGNIFIED.
3. SPINAL CORD AND MEDULLA OBLONGATA, WITH THEIR NERVES.
4. DIAGRAM OF STRUCTURE OF SPINAL CORD.
5. GENERAL VIEW OF THE NERVES GOING TO THE FACE, LUNGS, HEART, AND STOMACH.
6. SIDE VIEW OF THE BRAIN.
7. VERTICAL SECTION THROUGH THE SKIN, MAGNIFIED.
8. SURFACE VIEW OF THE SKIN, MAGNIFIED.
9. MODE OF CONNECTION OF THE NAIL.

Plate VIII.—The Senses.

Fig. 1. FRONT VIEW OF THE EYE-BALL AND TEAR APPARATUS.
2. MUSCLES OF THE EYE-BALL.
3. SECTION THROUGH THE EYE-BALL.
4. SURFACE VIEW OF THE RETINA, MAGNIFIED.
5. VERTICAL SECTION THROUGH THE RETINA, MAGNIFIED.
6. DIAGRAM OF VISUAL RAYS.
7. TONGUE, WITH ITS PAPILLÆ.
8. CONNECTION OF THE HAIR TO THE SKIN.
9. GENERAL VIEW OF THE EAR.
10. BONES OF THE TYMPANUM.
11. LABYRINTH OF THE EAR.
12. SECTION OF THE COCHLEA.
13. EXPANSE OF THE LAMINÆ.
14. VIEW OF VOCAL CORDS, WITH THEIR MUSCLES.
15. VERTICAL SECTION THROUGH THE NOSE, MOUTH, AND LARYNX.
16. SECTION THROUGH THE NOSE.

Second Edition.

THE HISTORICAL GEOGRAPHY

OF THE

CLANS OF SCOTLAND.

In Demy Quarto, Price, Full Bound Cloth, 7s. 6d.

By T. B. JOHNSTON, F.R.G.S. F.R.S.E. & F.S.A.S.

AND

Colonel JAMES A. ROBERTSON, F.S.A.S.

CONTENTS

REVIEWS.

"The Map bears evidence of careful preparation."—*Athenæum.*

"This is a valuable contribution to the history of the Scottish Highlands, and a delightful work for enthusiastic Highlanders."—*Early Review.*

"Antiquarians and students of Scottish history will seldom fall upon so many curious and interesting particulars as this most interesting folds supplies."—*Northern Herald.*

"The Map has been constructed with great labour and care, and is the first properly authenticated and accurate document of the kind that has been given to the public."—*N.B. Daily Mail.*

"Every Highland gentleman should at once provide himself with a copy of this graceful volume."—*The Courant.*

"Advantage has been taken of the publication of the clan map to republish a variety of interesting particulars as to the Highland Clans, which are not now of easy access to the ordinary reader."—*Greenock Advertiser.*

"The most useful of all companions to any history of Scotland, or of the Highlands."—*Edinburgh Quarterly Journal.*

GEOLOGICAL MAPS.

THE CABINET ATLAS

OF THE

ACTUAL GEOGRAPHY OF THE WORLD,

WITH

A COMPLETE INDEX TO EVERY PLACE

·IN THE ATLAS.

CONSTRUCTED BY

A. K. JOHNSTON, LL.D.

Royal Quarto, half-bound morocco, 26s., cloth, gilt, 21s.

CONTENTS.

Map		Map	
	Physical and Commercial Chart of the World (with Explanatory Notes), *Frontispiece.*	17	Greece.
1	World in Hemispheres.	18	Turkish Empire.
2	Europe.	19	Asia.
3	England.	20	India.
4	Scotland.	21	China and Japan.
5	Ireland.	22	Palestine.
6	France.	23	Oceania,
7	Netherlands and Belgium.	24	Australia.
8	Switzerland.	25	New Zealand.
9	Germany.	26	Africa.
10	South-West Germany.	27	Egypt and Abyssinia.
11	Austria.	28	South Africa.
12	Italy.	29	North America.
13	Spain and Portugal,	30	United States.
14	Sweden and Norway.	31	Dominion of Canada.
15	Denmark.	32	West India Islands.
16	Russia.	33	South America.
			Index.

Single Maps 6d. each.

THE

EDINBURGH EDUCATIONAL ATLAS
OF MODERN GEOGRAPHY.

IN 33 MAPS FULL COLOURED.

WITH INDEX.

Price, full bound cloth, 10s.

Single Maps 6d. each.

" The clearest and most satisfactory atlas we have yet seen for Schools."--*The Standard, 6th February* 1874.

ATLAS OF BRITISH HISTORY,

in Crown 8vo, Full Cloth, Containing 31 Maps, Printed in Colours, and Index to every name in the Atlas.

BY

KEITH JOHNSTON, LL.D.,

F.R.S.E., F.R.G.S., ETC.

UNIFORM WITH THE 'POLITICAL ATLAS' AND THE 'PHYSICAL ATLAS.'

Price 2s. 6d.

1. ENGLAND (Britannia), under the Romans.
2. SCOTLAND, under the Romans.
3. GALLIA (Roman Period).
4. ENGLAND (Saxon Period).
5. SCOTLAND (Saxon Period).
6. { FRANCE, North Part (Saxon-Norman Period). IRELAND (Tudor Period).
7. ENGLAND, and part of SCOTLAND (Norman and Plantagenet Period).
8. EUROPE (Norman and Plantagenet Period).
9. EUROPE, during the time of the Crusades.
10. FRANCE (Norman to Tudor Period), illustrating the French and English Wars.
11. ENGLAND, and part of SCOTLAND (York and Lancaster Period).
12. ENGLAND (Tudor Period).
13. } EUROPE during the time of the Reformation.
14. }
15. SCOTLAND (Tudor Period).
16. ENGLAND (Stuart Period).
17. SCOTLAND (Stuart Period).
18. IRELAND (Stuart and Brunswick Period).
19. } EUROPE (1600 to 1714), including Thirty Years War.
20. }
21. WORLD, showing Discoveries from XV. to XVII. Century.
22. ENGLAND (Brunswick Period).
23. { EUROPE, from 1715 to 1830, illustrating the Wars of the French
24. { Revolution, and Wars of Napoleon.
25. SCOTLAND (Brunswick Period).
26. NORTH AMERICA, illustrating the Conquest of Canada and the War of Independence.
27. EUROPE (Central), at the height of Napoleon's power, 1812.
28. INDIAN EMPIRE, from its foundation in 1757 to 1870.
29. Part of RUSSIA, to illustrate the Crimean War and the operations in the Baltic.
30. CENTRAL EUROPE, illustrating late Continental Wars, 1848-71, including recent changes on France.
31. WORLD, showing British Possessions and Dependencies.

Extracts from Reviews

OF THE

ATLAS OF BRITISH HISTORY,

UNIFORM WITH THE 'POLITICAL ATLAS' AND THE 'PHYSICAL ATLAS'

Containing 31 Maps (as on preceding page) Full Bound
Cloth, and an Index to every name in the Atlas.

'The necessity of maps to illustrate history is universally admitted, yet historical atlases are rare in this country. This renders the present one, containing 31 beautifully executed maps, all the more welcome, when we consider the moderate cost.'—*The Athenæum.*

'Here we may once more admit that a deficiency has been supplied. Cheap general atlases are now-a-days plentiful enough, but beyond this one we know of none at a reasonable price upon which a pupil could depend for real assistance in the study of history. No map likely to be met with in ordinary school histories is omitted, and the whole is executed in Messrs. Johnstons' well-known style.'—*The Standard.*

'There can be no doubt that a lamentable negligence has been shown in teaching this branch of knowledge (Historical Geography), but perhaps this may be partly accounted for by the want of a suitable means of imparting such instruction. But such an excuse as this will no longer be valid, for Mr. Keith Johnston's Atlas has been specially designed for supplying this want. To criticise its construction would be superfluous, inasmuch as Mr. Johnston's name is a guarantee for accuracy and excellence.'—*The Civil Service Gazette.*

'This atlas contains 31 excellent maps and a copious index, and will be found a valuable aid to the student of English History. We heartily recommend it to all teachers.'—*The Quarterly Journal of Education.*

'It would be difficult to overpraise this work, whether as a book of reference or as an assistant in the study of history. Nothing more useful of a geographical or historical character for school and study purposes can be well imagined.'—*The Scotsman.*

'The several changes which at certain convulsive periods like our own have occurred, were never so clearly and simply shown as in the Historical Atlas before us. In it we have a connected line of maps which illustrate, in such a manner as to be understood by schoolboys, the leading events of history. Although specially designed to elucidate British History—and for this purpose it is chiefly valuable—it also serves for a course of modern European history, "in sufficient detail for all ordinary purposes." The price of the atlas—less than one penny for each map—will surely make the book have a great circulation—as it deserves.'—*The Bookseller.*

KEITH JOHNSTON'S
SMALLER SCHOOL ATLASES
OF
POLITICAL GEOGRAPHY.
Printed in Colours.

SIXPENNY ATLAS.

In Wrapper.

CONTENTS.

1 Hemispheres.
2 Europe.
3 England.
4 Scotland.
5 Ireland.
6 S. W. Europe.
7 Asia.
8 Africa.
9 North America.
10 South America.
11 Palestine.

SHILLING ATLAS.

Cloth Back.

CONTENTS.

1 World.
2 Europe.
3 England.
4 Scotland.
5 Ireland.
6 France.
7 Central Europe.
8 Asia.
9 India.
10 Australia.
11 New Zealand.
12 Africa.
13 North America.
14 South America.
15 Palestine.

HALF-CROWN ATLAS.

Full Bound Cloth.

CONTENTS.

1 Hemispheres.
2 World (Mercator).
3 Europe.
4 British Isles.
5 England.
6 Manufacturing Districts of England, and Environs of London.
7 Scotland.
8 Ireland.
9 France.
10 Belgium and the Netherlands.
11 German Empire.
12 Austro-Hungarian Monarchy.
13 Switzerland.
14 Italy.
15 Spain and Portugal.
16 Sweden, Norway and Denmark.
17 Russia in Europe.
18 Greece.
19 Turkish Empire in Europe and Asia.
20 Asia.
21 Palestine.
22 India.
23 China and Japan.
24 Oceania.
25 Australia.
26 New Zealand.
27 Africa.
28 North America.
29 South America.
30 Canadian Dom.
31 United States and Mexico.

Index to every place in the Atlas.

All the special Maps are Illustrated by Plans of the Chief Towns or by Enlargements of important Districts.

Single Maps One Penny each, Coloured.

With the above Atlases of General or Political Geography are published others on the same plan on Physical and Historical Geography (one of Scripture Geography is in progress) ; and the Publishers venture to hope that they will thus, for the first time, place in the hands of many thousands of pupils a systematic and complete Series of Atlases, unrivalled for clearness of execution, accuracy of information, and moderation in price.

THE EDINBURGH QUARTO ATLAS,

Full Bound Cloth, Price One Shilling.

Containing 24 Maps beautifully printed in Colours, on substantial paper.

CONTENTS.

1 The Hemispheres.	9 Austria.	17 India.
2 Europe.	10 Spain.	18 Africa.
3 England.	11 Italy.	19 North America.
4 Scotland.	12 Switzerland.	20 Canada.
5 Ireland.	13 Norway and Sweden.	21 United States.
6 France.	14 Turkish Empire.	22 South America.
7 Belgium.	15 Asia.	23 Australia.
8 German Empire.	16 Palestine.	24 New Zealand.

Selections from a very great number of reviews of the above work.

"No school or school room should be without it."—*Northern Europe.*

"A Quarto Atlas, containing two dozen maps at a cost of less than a halfpenny each map, seems to us quite a marvel of cheapness."—*Glasgow Herald.*

"The Edinburgh Quarto Atlas can scarcely fail to become a favourite auxiliary in geographical study."—*Dundee Advertiser.*

"Of all the cheap school atlases issued by Messrs. Johnston, this is surely the cheapest and best."—*The Daily Review.*

"This is an admirable atlas for school purposes, or for easy general reference."—*The Fife Herald.*

"A small shilling atlas, well adapted for schools, and marvellously cheap."—*The Publishers Circular.*

THE EDINBURGH SIXPENNY QUARTO ATLAS

IN WRAPPER,

Containing 16 Maps beautifully printed in Colours, on substantial paper.

CONTENTS.

1 The Hemispheres.	7 England.	13 Canada.
2 Europe.	8 Scotland.	14 United States.
3 Asia.	9 Ireland.	15 Australia.
4 Africa.	10 Central Europe.	16 New Zealand.
5 North America.	11 India.	16 Palestine.
6 South America.		

Selections from a very great number of reviews of the above work.

"Sixteen correct, full-coloured maps on thick paper for sixpence! Is more needed to recommend an issue by Messrs. Johnston? Every teacher and geography class should have it."—*Northern Europe.*

"Cheapness and excellence combined seem to have reached an acme in this atlas."—*Art Journal.*

"The eminent geographers have omitted nothing that is really important to find in such an atlas."—*The Daily Review.*

"The number of cheap atlases already in the market is legion; but the merits of the "Sixpenny Quarto" will make for itself a place among them, while the name of the firm from which it emanates is a guarantee of its general correctness."—*Dundee Advertiser.*

"This is a marvellously cheap atlas for the use of children who are entering upon the study of geography. It contains no fewer than sixteen maps, drawn, printed and coloured, with all the accuracy and features which are characteristic of the works issued by this celebrated firm."—*North British Daily Mail.*

"Messrs. W. & A. K. Johnston have given us here a wonderful work, namely, an atlas with sixteen coloured maps for sixpence."—*Inverness Courier.*

PHYSICAL GEOGRAPHY.

SIXPENNY ATLAS.

In Wrapper.

CONTENTS.

1 Explanatory Diagrams.
2 Land and Water.
3 & 4 British Isles.
5 Palestine and Suez.
6 Winds and Storms.
7 & 8 Ocean Currents and River Systems.
9 & 10 Earthquakes and Volcanoes.
11 Climate, Isothermal Lines.

Hand-Book to Sixpenny Atlas of Physical Geography, Price 6d.

SHILLING ATLAS.

Cloth Back.

CONTENTS.

1 Explanatory Diagrams.
2 Land and Water.
3 & 4 Perspective View of the Globe.
5 & 6 British Isles.
7 Palestine and Suez.
8 Winds and Storms.
9 & 10 Ocean Currents and River Systems.
11 & 12 Earthquakes & Volcanoes.
13 & 14 Climate, Isotherms and Range Lines.
15 Races of Man.

Hand-Book to Shilling Atlas of Physical Geography, Price 1s.

HALF-CROWN ATLAS.

Full Bound Cloth.

CONTENTS.

1 Explanatory Diagrams
2 Land and Water.
3 & 4 Perspective View of the Globe.
5 & 6 Europe and Asia.
7 & 8 North and South America.
9 Africa.
10 Australasia.
11 & 12 British Isles (Hypsometrical)
13 Palestine and Suez.
14 British Isles, Geological.
15 & 16 Ocean Currents and River Systems.
17 Atlantic Ocean.
18 Mediterranean.
19 & 20 British Isles (Hydrographical).
21 Europe, River Systems.
22 Winds and Storms.
23 & 24 Climate, Isothermal and Range Lines.
25 & 26 Earthquakes and Volcanoes.
27 & 28 Distribution of useful Plants.
29 & 30 Distribution of chief Animals.
31 Races of Man.

WITH ANALYTICAL INDEX.

Hand-Book to Half Crown Physical Atlas, with full Analytical Index; Full Bound Cloth, 2s. 6d.

PHYSICAL GEOGRAPHY.

Price, Full Bound Cloth, 6s.

The above work consists of the Half Crown Atlas of Physical Geography and the Hand-Book bound together in one handsome volume.

POLITICAL and PHYSICAL ATLASES, Full Bound Morocco, 7s. 6d. each.

ATLAS

OF

THE BRITISH EMPIRE

IN

EUROPE, ASIA, OCEANIA, AFRICA, AND AMERICA.

WITH INDEX AND DESCRIPTIVE LETTERPRESS.

Price, Coloured, Full Bound Cloth, 1s. 6d.

CONTENTS.

OUTLINE ATLAS

OF

POLITICAL GEOGRAPHY.

UNIFORM WITH THE HALF-CROWN ATLAS OF

POLITICAL GEOGRAPHY.

Price, bound with Cloth Back, 1s. 6d.

CONTENTS.

The Geographical and Topographical features are printed in *Blue,*
the Names to be written by the Pupils in *Black Ink.*

A

PHYSICAL CHART OF THE WORLD.

By KEITH JOHNSTON, F.R.G.S.

Size, 4 feet 2 inches by 3 feet 6 inches.   Price, on Roller, Varnished, £1, 1s.

The main object of this chart is to give a clear view of the general nature of the land surface of the globe; to distinguish those belts which are mainly characterised by forest or desert, pasture land or barren tundra, and to show the extent of the icy caps of the polar regions. For each of the landscape zones a colouring has been chosen which may be considered as representative of its general aspect; thus, the equatorial regions of luxuriant tropical forest vegetation are shown in a bright green; the deserts of both hemispheres, in a hot dense tint; the forest lands of the temperate regions, in a dark sombre green; and the mossy tundra in grey; whilst the ice floes of the polar regions appear in white against the blue of the ocean colouring.

The limits of each of these different regions have been worked out with great labour and care, and thus the chart, as a whole, is believed to give a much more pleasing and instructive view of the general aspect of the globe, in some approach to its natural colouring, than any physical map hitherto published.

The landscape zones, besides being dependent on latitude, and on the shape of the continents, are conditioned in their form both by the elevation of the land and the unequal distribution of warmth and moisture. To aid the explanation of the irregularities of shape introduced by the former cause, contour lines showing the level of 2000 and 5000 feet above the sea have been drawn with the greatest attainable accuracy; besides which, the observed elevations of upwards of 650 mountains, lakes, passes, and towns, have been set down upon the map; and, to illustrate the latter cause, the ocean currents, as main agents in the transference of heat and cold, have been delineated, the warmer and colder ocean streams being distinguished by different tints. Still further to assist the explanation of the main subject, four smaller diagrams, showing the distribution of temperature over land and sea, and of the direction of the winds in relation to barometric pressure, for each of the extreme seasons of the year—the months of January and July—have been appended to the chief map.

As of great interest in the physical geography of the globe, though subordinate to the chief object of the map, the depths of the ocean bed, so far as these have been ascertained by sounding, the great submarine banks, the distribution of coral reefs, the chief volcanic mountains, the points to which the great rivers are navigable, and the salt lakes of the continental drainage basins as distinguished from the fresh lakes which drain to the sea are subjects also illustrated by this chart.

COMPANION TO THE ABOVE,

THE SURFACE ZONES OF THE GLOBE.

WITH 6 COLOURED VIEWS AND 2 COLOURED MAPS.

By KEITH JOHNSTON, F.R.G.S.

Crown 8vo, Full Bound Cloth.   Price 3s. 6d.

NEW EDITION OF
JOHNSTON'S COMMERCIAL AND LIBRARY

CHART OF THE WORLD,
ON MERCATOR'S PROJECTION, 1874.

This well known and valuable Work, of which many thousand copies have been purchased by the principal mercantile establishments of Europe, India, and the Colonies, has, in accordance with the rapid progress of geographical science, been thoroughly revised and corrected up to the present year, 1874. It exhibits the most recent changes in political boundaries: In Europe, the new German Empire, the altered frontier of France, consequent on the results of the Franco-Germanic War, the kingdom of Italy, etc. In Asia, the encroachments of Russia on the Chinese territory in the basin of the Amur, with the new posts on the Pacific; the extension of British territory in India, and the new French Colony of Lower Cochin China. In Africa, Speke, Grant, and Baker's discoveries of the sources of the Nile, and the explorations of Barth, Burton, and Livingstone, in Central and Southern Africa. In America, the Colonies of British Columbia, Vancouver Island, and Sitkhen, with all the new territories of the United States. In Australasia, Queensland, discoveries in the interior of Australia, and the French Colony of New Caledonia.

Besides the information usually given in a Chart of the World, this Map contains the following: —

1. ENLARGED MAP OF EUROPE, showing to colours the countries comprised in the new German Empire, the Railways and Canals of Continental States, and the relative importance of the principal towns.

2. ENLARGED MAPS OF THE COLONIES of New South Wales and Victoria, the Cape Colony, Malta, etc.; the Railway across the Isthmus of Panama, the proposed Inter-oceanic canal through Central America, with enlarged plans of the more important commercial ports in the world. A distinctive feature of the Chart is, that Britain and all her possessions are shown in one uniform red colour, which explains at once the vast extent of British territory, and facilitates the finding of remote dependencies.

3. LENGTH OF DAY. A scale extending from the Equator to the North Pole, showing the comparative duration of the longest day from sunrise to sunset, from 12 hours to 5 months.

4. TIME TABLE. Figures on the lower margin of the Map, showing the difference of time between that of the meridian of Greenwich and any place on the globe, to the east or west of it.

5. CURRENTS OF THE OCEAN. The limits of the currents, as far as known, are all defined by shading. Arrows indicate their direction, and their rate of motion in 24 hours is given in nautical miles.

6. FUCUS BANK. The Fucus Bank of Corvo and Flores (Sargasso or Grassy Sea), a mass of sea weed floating in the Atlantic Ocean, so thick as frequently to retard the progress of vessels, and so extensive as to cover a surface equal to 260,000 square miles.

7. STEAM-PACKET ROUTES. The tracks followed by steam-packets all over the world.

8. SOUNDINGS. The depth of the sea, and minimum depth of water on sandbanks, are given in fathoms. The position of the greatest depth ever sounded (twenty 5½ miles) is marked in the South Atlantic Ocean, between St. Helena and the coast of Brazil.

9. ICE. The limits of permanent and floating ice in summer and winter, showing the danger to navigation arising from ice-fields, especially in crossing the Atlantic Ocean.

10. NAVAL ENGAGEMENTS. The positions are marked by two cross guns, and a note gives the date of the action.

11. TELEGRAPHIC COMMUNICATIONS over the globe, printed in red.

Size—9 Feet by 6 Feet 8 Inches

Price *Coloured and Varnished, on a Mahogany Roller, or in the Mount Case for Drawing room or Library, £3, 3s.*

Price—*Framed and Varnished, with Gilt Bead, £4, 10s.*

A NEW EDITION OF

KEITH JOHNSTON'S

FOUR-SHEET MAP OF EUROPE

AND ADJACENT COUNTRIES,

Extending from Iceland on the North, to Cairo on the South ; from Khiva on the East, to the Atlantic Ocean on the West. This Map contains the latest **Territorial Divisions**, and, amongst other details, shews all the **Railways**, including the most recently opened in Russia. The heights of the more important **Mountains** are given in English feet—distances from Port to Port in miles ; the lines of **Submarine Telegraphs** and **Fortified Towns** are shown, and the dates and sites of **Battles**, etc., etc., indicated.

The Map measures 4 feet 4 inches by 3 feet 7 inches, and is clearly and carefully coloured.

Price, mounted on Cloth on Stained Wood Rollers,

varnished	£1	1	0
In Quarto Cloth Case, titled on side, . .	1	1	0
On Mahogany Rollers, bound with silk and varnished,	1	10	0
In 8vo Case, in four sheets for travelling, titled, .	1	10	0
On Spring Roller, with Mahogany Case, .	8	8	0

A LIBRARY AND OFFICE

MAP OF THE BRITISH ISLES.

This large Map, on the scale of 14 miles to one inch, has been specially prepared for the Counting-house and Library, and will be found of the greatest service to all those who require to travel by rail, or who have to transmit goods from one part of the kingdom to another.

The extensive and intricate system of **Railway Lines** throughout the Empire has been laid down with great care; and to render it perfectly distinct and easily followed, the Railways are printed in bright red over the Map. The **Counties** in the three countries are clearly coloured ; the **Sea Tracks** from the more important ports are given, as well as the Telegraphs from coast to coast.

A **Section** of England from the Menai Straits to the English Channel is also shown, as well as Maps of the Channel Islands, and the Island of Heligoland.

The Map possesses the great advantage over separate maps, in showing the three kingdoms on the same scale, and in their relative positions, a great advantage in a country where so much intercommunication exists.

Size, 4 feet 6 inches by 3 feet 10 inches.

Price Coloured, on Roller and Varnished, £1, 1s.
Other Styles of Mounting charged at the same rates as those of
" *Europe* " *given above.*

ILLUSTRATIONS OF THE VARIOUS MODES OF MOUNTING MAPS ON SPRING ROLLERS.

1.

Single Map (Large Library Size) on Spring Roller (no Case), £6, 16s. 6d.
Size of Map, 6 feet 2 inches by 4 feet 6 inches.
The above in Patent Window-Blind Mounting, £4, 10s.

11.

Single Map (Large Library Size) on Spring Roller, with Mahogany or Oak
Case, £10, 10s. 6d.

3.

Oak Stand, with Six Library Maps, £77.
„   Case,   „   £80.

METRIC SYSTEM.

A Synoptic Table, *with Diagrams*, showing the Actual Size of Weights and Measures, by C. H. DOWLING, C.E., *with Hand-Book*, by JAMES YATES, Esq., M.A., etc., etc.

SIZE— 5 FEET BY 4 FEET 2 INCHES.

PRICE—Coloured on Cloth and Rollers .		£0 15	0
,, ,, Varnished,		0 17	0
,, In 4to Portfolio, .		0 15	0

REDUCTION OF THE ABOVE, Size 33 by 27 inches.

PRICE—Coloured on Cloth and Rollers, .	.	£0 5	0
,, ,, Varnished, .		0 6	0
With Hand-Book.			

A MAP OF THE TEA-PRODUCING COUNTRIES

OF

NORTH EASTERN BENGAL,

INCLUDING THE

VALLEY OF THE BRAHMAHPOOTRA, ASSAM, CACHAR, ETC.,

Embracing the entire country between the Eastern Bengal Railway at Kooshtet, and the frontier station of Sudiya, on the Brahmahpootra;

SHOWING THE POSITIONS OF THE PRINCIPAL

TEA GARDENS,

WITH NAMES OF PROPRIETORS.

THE

Jute-producing Districts and Coal Fields are also shown.

COMPILED FROM EXISTING GOVERNMENT SURVEYS, AND FROM PERSONAL OBSERVATIONS BY

MAJOR BRIGGS,

Superintending Engineer, Assam.

SIZE OF MAP 3 FEET 3 INCHES BY 2 FEET 3 INCHES. SCALE 12 MILES TO AN INCH. Engraved on Copper, Printed and Coloured in the finest style.

Price, Coloured, on Cloth and Rollers (varnished), or folded in case,						£1 11	6
,, *on Sheets, Coloured,*	.	.	.	.	.	1 1	0

FACSIMILE OF GORDON OF ROTHIEMAY'S

BIRD'S-EYE VIEW OF EDINBURGH, 1647,

WITH AN HISTORICAL NOTICE BY DAVID LAING, ESQ., LL.D., F.S.A.S.

India Paper Proof,	.	.	.	.	.	£2 2	0
Plain Proof, .	.	.	.	.	.	1 1	0
Prints from Stone;	.	.	.	.	.	0 10	6

MOUNTED ON CLOTH, 4to CASE.

Plain Proof, 4to morocco case, gilt, .	.	.	1 15	6
Prints from Stone, 4to cloth case,	.	.	1 0	0

FRAMED WITH GLASS.

India Proof, .	.	.	.	.	3 3 0
Plain Proof, .	.	.	.	.	2 2 0
Prints from Stone,	.	.	.	.	1 11 6

A SKETCH MAP OF THE

LAKE REGION OF EASTERN AFRICA,

Showing Dr. LIVINGSTONE'S Discoveries and Routes from 1866
to 1872, and Mr. STANLEY'S Route from Zanzibar.

By KEITH JOHNSTON, F.R.G.S.

Price 1s. 6d. ; *or on Cloth and in Case,* 3s. 6d.

MAP OF THE LAKE REGION OF EASTERN AFRICA,

Showing LIVINGSTONE'S Researches to 1870.

WITH MEMOIR.

Price 5s.

MAP OF THE SUEZ CANAL, WITH SECTIONS.

Price, Coloured, 1s. 6d.

EMIGRATION MAPS.

A MAP OF THE DOMINION OF CANADA,

Comprising the Provinces of Ontario, Quebec, Nova Scotia, and New Brunswick; Prince
Edward Island, Cape Breton Island, and the recently formed Province of Manitoba.
Sub-divided by colours into counties and townships, and showing all the Railways, Canals,
latest settlements, etc., etc. Size, 4 feet 2 inches by 3 feet 6 inches. Price, full coloured,
on Rollers, for the Counting-house, or in Case for the Emigrant, 21s.

A MAP OF AUSTRALIA

From the most recent official Surveys and other documents, showing the Boundaries,
Town, Ports, Harbours, and Settlements of Queensland, New South Wales, Victoria, South
Australia, West Australia, Alexandra Land, and Tasmania, with the Track Routes of Stuart,
Burke, Wills, etc., etc. Size, 4 feet 7 inches by 3 feet 6 inches. Price, full coloured, on
Rollers, for the Counting-house, or in Case for the Emigrant, 21s.

A MAP OF NEW ZEALAND

Showing, on a clear and distinct scale, 18½ miles to an inch, the Provinces of Auckland,
Taranaki, Wellington, Hawke Bay, Nelson, Marlborough, Canterbury, Westland, Otago,
and Southland, with the Recent Discoveries in the Southern Alps, the New Gold Fields,
Railways, etc. Price, full coloured, on Rollers, for the Counting-house, or in Case for the
Emigrant, 21s.

A MAP OF THE PACIFIC OCEAN,

Showing all the principal Ports of Australia, New Zealand, North and South America, China,
Japan, and the Islands of Oceania, Polynesia, and Micronesia; with Ocean Routes and Time
on the Voyage. Size, 4 feet 2 inches by 3 feet 6 inches. Price, full coloured, on Rollers, for
the Counting-house, or in Case for the Emigrant, 21s.

Separate Maps, carefully Coloured, with Statistical Notes, Distances and Duration
of Voyages from England.

AUSTRALIA.

1. Queensland.   2. New South Wales, Victoria, and South Australia.

NEW ZEALAND.

1. The Provinces of Auckland, Wellington, Taranaki, New Plymouth, and Hawke Bay.
2. Nelson, Marlborough, Canterbury.   3. Otago, Canterbury, and Southland
Size, 25 by 20 inches.   Price, in Cloth Cover, coloured, 3s. 6d. ; or on Cloth, in case, 5s. 6d
each.

NEW MAPS OF PORTIONS OF SCOTLAND.

(SEE ALSO PAGES 13 AND 21.)

MAPS OF THE COUNTIES OF SCOTLAND,

From New Surveys.

THE COUNTY OF SUTHERLAND.

From an entirely New Survey, executed for his Grace the Duke of Sutherland, on a Scale of Half an Inch to a Mile.

Price, on Rollers, varnished, 18s. 6d. ; or in Case for the Pocket, 16s.

THE COUNTY OF WIGTON.

Reduced from the Ordnance Survey, on a Scale of One and a Half Inches to the Mile.

Price, on Mahogany Rollers, Varnished, or in Case for the Pocket, £2, 2s., or on Stained Wood Rollers, Unvarnished, £1, 11s. 6d. ; Varnished, £1, 18s.

GREENWOOD'S COUNTY MAPS.

FIFE AND KINROSS.

On 4 Imperial Sheets, 20s.   On Cloth, in Case, 30s.   Rollers, varnished, 35s.

EDINBURGH.

On 2 Imperial Sheets, 10s.   On Cloth, in Case, 16s.   Rollers, varnished, 18s. 6d.

HADDINGTON.

On 2 Imperial Sheets, 10s.   On Cloth, in Case, 16s.   Rollers, varnished, 18s. 6d.

BERWICK.

On 2 Imperial Sheets, 10s.   On Cloth, in Case, 15s.   Rollers, varnished, 18s. 6d.

SCHOOL BOARD COUNTY MAPS.

A SERIES OF MAPS OF THE COUNTIES OF SCOTLAND, SHOWING RAILWAYS, ETC. ; WITH SHORT DESCRIPTIVE NOTE APPENDED TO EACH. PREPARED TO SUIT PUPILS IN MEETING THE REQUIREMENTS OF THE NEW EDUCATION CODE FOR SCOTLAND.

Price 3s. 4d. per 100, Coloured ; smaller quantities 2d. each.

Now ready.

EDINBURGHSHIRE, FIFE AND KINROSS, STIRLING AND DUMBARTONSHIRE.

ROAD MAP OF THE COUNTIES OF STIRLING AND DUMBARTON.

With the Railways.   Size, 16 by 13 inches.   Price, in Case, 2s. 6d.

KNOX'S MAPS OF THE BASINS OF THE FORTH AND TAY. .

On a Scale of half an inch to a Mile.

The above two maps include parts of the adjoining Counties, and contain the Railways, Roads, Elevations, etc.

Price, each on Rollers, varnished, 7s. 6d. ; on Cloth, in Case, 5s. ; in Wrapper, 2s. 6d.

3

PLANS OF THE CITY OF EDINBURGH.

NEW EDITION, 1870.

JOHNSTON'S OFFICE OR LIBRARY PLAN OF THE CITY.

From *actual Survey*, by A. LANCEFIELD, Esq., C.E.

On a Scale of 13½ inches to a mile.

Size, 5 feet 6 inches by 4 feet 5 inches.

The limits of the Plan are those of the Parliamentary Boundaries of Edinburgh and Leith, and it can be had divided into Parishes, Police Wards, Municipal Districts, etc., or Coloured to Order, to exhibit particular properties, etc.

Price, Handsomely Coloured, Mounted on Mahogany Rollers, or in Morocco Quarto Case, £2, 12s. 6d.

Ditto, Framed and Varnished, with Gilt Bead, £3, 17s. 6d.

In 16 Sheets, Coloured, in Portfolio, £1, 7s. 6d.   Single Sheets, 1s. 6d.

KIRKWOOD'S PLAN OF THE CITY OF EDINBURGH.

Size, 5 feet 6 inches by 4 feet 10 inches.

Price, on Mahogany Rollers, £2, 12s. 6d.

This Plan was first published in 1815, and is valuable for showing the changes which have taken place in the city and its vicinity. It contains the names of Proprietors, and shows the Feuing Plans for the extension of the New Town, Leith, etc.

JOHNSTON'S ONE-SHEET PLAN OF THE CITY.

Price, Mounted in Case for Tourists, 1s.   Environs of do., 1s. 6d.

ROAD AND RAILWAY MAP OF THE COUNTY OF EDINBURGH.

With portions of the adjoining Counties, Price 6d. in Wrapper.

KNOX'S ENVIRONS OF THE CITY OF EDINBURGH.

With all the Railways on the Scale of one and a half inches to a mile.

Size, 22 by 17 inches.   Price, in Wrapper, 1s. 6d.

RAILWAY MAPS PRINTED IN COLOURS.

Britain, in Wrapper, 1s. 6d.   Scotland, in Wrapper, 1s.   Scotland, in Wrapper, 6d.

THE

NAUTICAL GUIDE TO THE FORTH AND TAY.

A correct Chart of these Rivers, from ST. ABB'S HEAD to STIRLING, and from the BELL ROCK to PERTH.

From the most recent Admiralty Surveys; accompanied by descriptive letterpress and sailing directions, storm-signals, signals for depth of water, buoys, etc.

Price, Coloured, Mounted on Cloth, ...	4s. 6d.
,, Mounted on Cloth, on Black Rollers, . .	10s. 6d.
,, Mounted on Cloth, on Mahogany Rollers, .	12s. 6d.

LARGE OUTLINE CHARTS OF THE WORLD.

1.—IN TWENTY SHEETS.

FOR THE LECTURE ROOM AND EXHIBITION HALL.

Size, when joined, about 15 feet by 12 feet.

Price, in Sheets, Plain, £5—or £7, Mounted in Three Pieces to join up.

This Chart, which is accurately constructed in a bold deckled style, is so arranged that, by means of colours, it may be readily made available for the illustration of any branch of Physical Geography or Natural History. It contains Rivers, Lakes, and Sea Coasts; Lines of Mean Summer, Mean Winter, and Mean Annual Temperature, distinguished by different marks; the Principal Cities and Towns on the Globe, to which are attached in figures, the Summer, Winter, and Annual Temperatures. The Names of Places, etc., are so small as not to be obtrusive, yet so distinct as to be easily read when near.

2.—A SKELETON MAP OF THE WORLD,

IN FOUR SHEETS.

Size, 6 feet by 4 feet 4 inches.

WITH THE PRINCIPAL RIVERS, MOUNTAIN-RANGES, AND CITIES.

FOR THE USE OF THE NATURALIST AND STATIST, OR FOR ANY SCIENTIFIC PURPOSE.

Price, in Sheets, Plain, 14s.; or 30s. on Cloth and Roller.

MAP OF EUROPE.

On 4 Sheets Coloured, for Educational purposes. The Rivers and Mountains boldly drawn, and the names of places few and carefully selected.

SIZE—6 FEET BY 5 FEET 6 INCHES. Price on Roller, Varnished, £1, 10s.

HEBREW MAP OF PALESTINE.

SIZE—29 BY 23 INCHES.

Price, Coloured, on Roller, Varnished, 4s. 6d., Unvarnished, 4s.

Black Boards, Ball Frames, Pointers, etc.

MAPS, DIAGRAMS, AND OTHER ILLUSTRATIONS FOR THE LECTURE ROOM,

OF ANY SIZE, DRAWN AND MOUNTED ON CLOTH AND ROLLERS.

PENMANSHIP.

A large Sheet of Ornamental Writing for use in Schools. Price 1s. 6d.

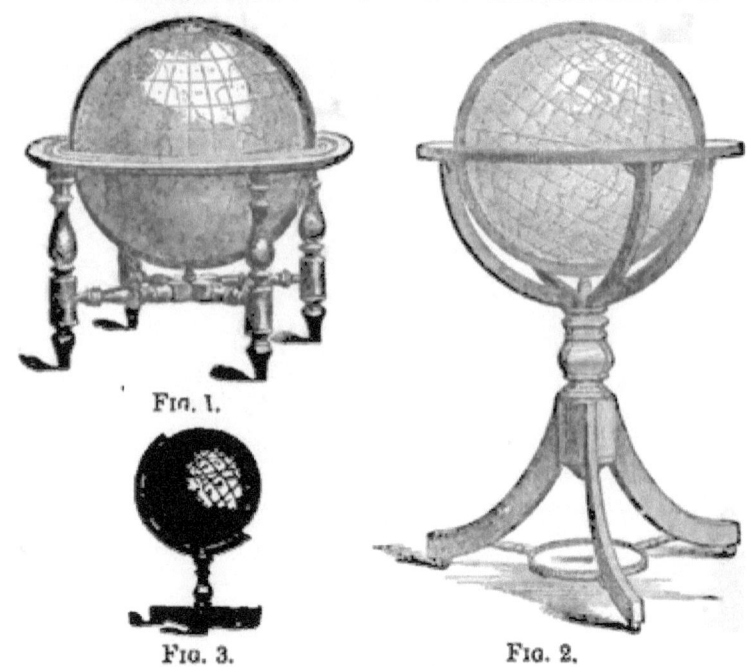

FIG. 1.

FIG. 3.

FIG. 2.

JOHNSTON'S

TERRESTRIAL AND CELESTIAL GLOBES,

WITH THE MOST RECENT DISCOVERIES.

						£	s	d
30 Inch Globe, with Varnished Stand (Terrestrial only),				Fig. 1,	£8	18	6
18	,,	,,	Low Black Stand,	Each,	,, 1,	5	5	0
18	,,	,,	Low Mahogany Stand,	,,	,, 1,	5	15	6
18	,,	,,	High Mahogany Stand,	,,	,, 2,	7	17	6
12	,,	,,	Low Black Stand,	,,	,, 1,	2	12	6
12	,,	,,	High Mahogany Stand,	,,	,, 2,	3	13	6
6	,,	,,	Low Black Stand,	,,	,, 1,	1	5	0
6	,,	,,	Semi Meridian,	,,	,, 3,	0	15	0
3	,,	,,	Full Mounted	,,	,, 1,	0	15	0
3	,,	,,	Semi Meridian,	,,	,, 3,	0	8	6
2½	,,	,,	do. do.	,,	,, 3,	0	6	0
1½	,,	,,	do. do.	,,	,, 3,	0	3	6

When packing cases are returned *and received*, a small charge only is made for the use of them. The Publishers do not, under *any circumstances*, hold themselves responsible for damage Globes may sustain after leaving their premises.

Quadrants, 30 inch. 8s. 6d.; 18 inch, 8s. 6d.; 12 inch, 3s. 6d.

OLD GLOBES RE-COVERED.

							£	s	d	
18 Inch Globes		.	.	.	.	.	£2	15	6	each
12	...	.	.	.	.	.	1	6	6	..

Repairs on Stand charged in addition according to Work.

Geographical and Educational Works

SUPPLIED BY

W. & A. K. JOHNSTON, EDINBURGH AND LONDON.

--- ∞:✕:∞ ---

NEW EDITION, 1874.
DEDICATED BY SPECIAL PERMISSION TO HER MAJESTY.

THE ONLY ATLAS FOR WHICH A PRIZE MEDAL WAS AWARDED
AT THE INTERNATIONAL EXHIBITION, 1862.

THE ROYAL
ATLAS OF MODERN GEOGRAPHY.

In a Series of entirely Original and Authentic Maps.

BY

A. K. JOHNSTON, F.R.S.E., F.R.G.S.

Author of the 'Physical Atlas,' etc.

*With a complete Index of easy reference to each Map, comprising nearly
150,000 Places contained in this Atlas.*

Imperial Folio, hf.-bd. in russia or morocco, £5, 15s. 6d.

CONTENTS.

<table>
<tr><td>Plate.</td><td></td><td></td><td></td></tr>
<tr><td></td><td>North Polar Chart, Frontispiece.</td><td></td><td></td></tr>
<tr><td>1.</td><td>The World (in Hemispheres),</td><td>With Index to 1400 Places.</td><td></td></tr>
<tr><td>2.</td><td>Chart of the World on Mercator's } Projection,</td><td>,,</td><td>1340 ,,</td></tr>
<tr><td>*3.</td><td>Europe,</td><td>,,</td><td>2120 ,,</td></tr>
<tr><td>4.</td><td>Basin of the North Atlantic Ocean,</td><td>,,</td><td>1010 ,,</td></tr>
<tr><td>*5, 6.</td><td>England (Two Sheets),</td><td>,,</td><td>10,600 ,,</td></tr>
<tr><td>*7, 8.</td><td>Scotland (Two Sheets),</td><td>,,</td><td>9250 ,,</td></tr>
<tr><td>*9.</td><td>Ireland,</td><td>,,</td><td>5270 ,,</td></tr>
<tr><td>*10.</td><td>France in Departments,</td><td>,,</td><td>4400 ,,</td></tr>
<tr><td>*11.</td><td>Spain and Portugal,</td><td>,,</td><td>4100 ,,</td></tr>
<tr><td>*12.</td><td>Basin of Mediterranean Sea,</td><td>,,</td><td>2170 ,,</td></tr>
<tr><td>*13, 14.</td><td>Northern Italy and Southern Italy } (Two Sheets),</td><td>,,</td><td>6230 ,,</td></tr>
<tr><td>*15.</td><td>Switzerland, and the Alps of Savoy } and Piedmont,</td><td>,,</td><td>4997 ,,</td></tr>
<tr><td>*16. {</td><td>Belgium, } One
The Netherlands, } Sheet</td><td>,,
,,</td><td>2100 ,,
2200 ,,</td></tr>
<tr><td>17. {</td><td>Denmark and Iceland, } One }
Hanover, Brunswick, Mecklen- } Sheet }
burg, Oldenburg, &c.</td><td>,,
,,</td><td>2200 ,,
1180 ,,</td></tr>
<tr><td>*18.</td><td>Empire of Germany, South West part,</td><td>,,</td><td>4470 ,,</td></tr>
<tr><td>*19.</td><td>Do. do. Northern part,</td><td>,,</td><td>2550 ,,</td></tr>
<tr><td>*20, 21.</td><td>Austro-Hungarian Monarchy (Two Sheets),</td><td>,,</td><td>6300 ,,</td></tr>
<tr><td>22.</td><td>Turkey in Europe,</td><td>,,</td><td>2280 ,,</td></tr>
<tr><td>23.</td><td>Greece, etc.,</td><td>,,</td><td>2187 ,,</td></tr>
<tr><td>*24.</td><td>Sweden and Norway (Scandinavia),</td><td>,,</td><td>1630 ,,</td></tr>
<tr><td>25.</td><td>Basin of the Baltic Sea,</td><td>,,</td><td>1890 ,,</td></tr>
<tr><td>26.</td><td>European Russia,</td><td>,,</td><td>3070 ,,</td></tr>
<tr><td>27.</td><td>South-West Russia,</td><td>,,</td><td>3740 ,,</td></tr>
<tr><td>28.</td><td>Asia,</td><td>,,</td><td>3900 ,,</td></tr>
<tr><td>29.</td><td>Turkey in Asia (Asia Minor) and } Transcaucasia,</td><td>,,</td><td>2850 ,,</td></tr>
<tr><td>*30.</td><td>Palestine,</td><td>,,</td><td>3100 ,,</td></tr>
<tr><td>31.</td><td>Persia and Afghanistan,</td><td>,,</td><td>2150 ,,</td></tr>
<tr><td>*32, 33.</td><td>India (Two Sheets),</td><td>,,</td><td>7500 ,,</td></tr>
<tr><td>*34.</td><td>China and Japan,</td><td>,,</td><td>2420 ,,</td></tr>
<tr><td>35.</td><td>Oceania,</td><td>,,</td><td>2500 ,,</td></tr>
<tr><td>*36.</td><td>South Australia, New South Wales, } and Victoria,</td><td>,,</td><td>1980 ,,</td></tr>
</table>

Plate.		With Index to the Places.
37.	Africa	" 1340 "
34.	North Western Africa, } One Sheet	" 126 "
	Southern Africa, }	
39, 44.	Egypt, Nubia, Abyssinia, and Arabia Petræa (Two Sheets)	" 540 "
41.	North America	" 1740 "
42, 43.	Dominion of Canada, New } Two Sheets }	" 270 "
	Brunswick, Nova Scotia, } and Newfoundland	
44, 45.	United States of North America (Two Sheets)	" 5573 "
44.	West Indies and Central America,	" 1170 "
47, 48.	South America, (Two Sheets)	" 5400 "

*Each Plate may be had separately, with its Index, price 1s.; and those marked thus * mounted on Linen, in each case for the pocket, if in One Sheet, 2s. 6d.; in Two Sheets, 4s.*

NEW EDITION, 1874.

DEDICATED BY SPECIAL PERMISSION TO H. R. H. THE PRINCE OF WALES.

THE HANDY ROYAL ATLAS

OF

MODERN GEOGRAPHY.

A UNIFORM SERIES OF NEW AND ACCURATE MAPS.

Accompanied by a Complete Index of upwards of 58,000 Places contained in the Atlas, and referred to by Initial Letters, with position in Longitude and Latitude,

BY

A. KEITH JOHNSTON, LL.D.

Imperial Quarto, half-bound morocco, gilt, £2, 12s. 6d.

CONTENTS.

Map		Map	
	North Polar Chart, *Frontispiece.*	23	Asia.
1	The World in Hemispheres.	24	Turkey in Asia.
2	Mercator's Chart of the World.	25	Palestine.
3	Europe.	26	Persia, etc.
4	England, North.	27	Indian Empire, North.
5	Do. South.	28	Do. South.
6	Scotland, North.	29	China and Japan.
7	Do. South.	30	Oceania.
8	Ireland.	31	Australia (General Map).
9	France.	32	New South Wales, Victoria, etc.
10	Spain and Portugal.	33	New Zealand.
11	Basin of the Mediterranean.	34	Africa.
12	Italy.	35	Do. North and South.
13	Switzerland and Savoy.	36	Egypt, etc.
14	Belgium and the Netherlands.	37	Nubia and Abyssinia.
15	Denmark, Schleswig-Holstein, etc.	38	North America.
16	Empire of Germany (South West part).	39	Dominion of Canada (Western Sheet).
17	Empire of Germany (Northern Part).	40	Do. Do. (Eastern Sheet).
18	Austro-Hungarian Monarchy.	41	United States, West.
19	Turkey in Europe.	42	Do. East.
20	Greece.	43	West India Islands.
21	Sweden and Norway.	44	South America, North.
22	Russia in Europe.	45	Do. South.

Single Sheets 1s. 6d. each, coloured.

New and Enlarged Edition, Imperial 4to, half-bound 8vo, 12s. 6d.,
half-bound 4to, 25s.   Printed in Colours.

SCHOOL ATLAS

OF

General and Descriptive Geography.

By A. KEITH JOHNSTON, LL.D.

Exhibiting the Actual and Comparative Extent of all the Countries in the World, with their Present Political Divisions.

Constructed with a special view to the purposes of sound instruction.

CONTENTS.

New and Enlarged Edition, Imperial 4to, half-bound 8vo, 12s. 6d.,
half-bound 4to, 25s.

School Atlas of Physical Geography.

By A. KEITH JOHNSTON, LL.D.

In this Atlas of Physical Geography the subject is treated in a more simple and elementary manner than in the previous works of the Author—the object being to convey broad and general ideas on the form and structure of our Planet, and the principal phenomena affecting its outer crust.   Printed in Colours.

CONTENTS.

New & Enlarged Edition, Imp. 4to, half-bound 8vo, 12s. 6d., half-bound, 4to, 25s.

School Atlas of Classical Geography.

By A. KEITH JOHNSTON, LL.D.

Comprising, in Twenty-Three Plates, Maps and Plans of all the Important Countries and Localities Referred to by Classical Authors.

Constructed from the best Materials, and embodying the Results of the most recent Investigations. With a full Index.

Map   *CONTENTS.*

1. Plan of Rome, and Illustrations of Classical Sites.
2. The World as known to the Ancients.
3. Map of the outer Geography of the Odyssey.
4. Orbis Terrarum (et Orb. Homeri, Herodoti, Democriti, Strabonis, Ptolemæi).
5. Hispania.
6. Gallia.
7. Insulæ Britannicæ (et Brit. Strabonis, Brit. Ptolemæi, etc.).
8. Germania, Vindelicia, Rhætia, et Noricum.
9. Pannonia, Dacia, Illyricum, Mœsia, Macedonia, et Thracia.
10. Italia Superior et Corsica.
11. Italia Inferior, Sicilia, et Sardinia (et Campania, Syracusæ, Roma).
12. Imperium Romanum (et Imp. Rom. Orient. et Occid.)
13. Græcia (et Athenæ, Marathon, Thermopylæ).
14. Peloponnesus, Attica, Bœotia, Phocis, Ætolia, et Acarnania.
15. Græcia e Bello Peloponnesiaco, inque ad Philippum II. (et Mantinea, Leuctra Platæa).
16. Asia Minor (et Campus Trojæ, Bosporus, Troas Insula, etc.).
17. Syria et Palestina (et Hierosolyma, etc.).
18. Armenia, Mesopotamia, Babylonia, Assyria (et Iter Xenophontis).
19. Regnum Alexandri Magni (et Granicus, Issus, Arbela).
20. Persis et India (et India Ptolemæi).
21. Ægyptus, Arabia, et Æthiopia (et Ægyptus Inferior).
22. Africa (et Carthago, Alexandria, Numidia, et Africa Propria).
23. Europe, showing the general direction of the Barbarian Inroads during the Decline and Fall of the Roman Empire.

Index.

New & Enlarged Edition, Imp. 4to, half-bound 8vo, 12s. 6d. half-bound 4to, 25s.

School Atlas of Astronomy.

By A. KEITH JOHNSTON, LL.D.

With Notes and Descriptive Letterpress to each Plate, embodying all recent Discoveries in Astronomy. Twenty Plates, printed in colours, by a new process.

Plate   *CONTENTS.*

1. The Celestial Sphere—Refraction—Parallax—Aberration of Light—Phases of the Moon—of the Inferior Planets, and of Saturn's Ring.
2. Axial Rotation of the Earth—Day and Night—Her Annual Revolution in the Ecliptic—The Seasons—The Tides.
3. The Solar Spots—Rotation of the Sun—His apparent Magnitude from the various Planets—The Zodiacal Light.
4. Telescopic appearance of the Moon.
5. Eclipses of the Sun, and Phenomena attending them.
6. Eclipses of the Moon.
7. The Solar or Planetary System.
8. Position of the Earth in the Solar System.
9. Transits of Mercury—Telescopic appearance of the Planets—Their relative dimensions.
10. Comets.
11. Double Stars—Binary Systems—Coloured Stars—Clusters—Distribution of the Stars—The Via Lactea.
12. Nebulæ.
13. Tracks of Meteors, 13th and 14th November 1866, and Diagram.
14. Spectrum Analysis applied to the Stars.
15. to 20, Maps of the stars.

New and Cheaper Edition, demy 4to, half-bound 8vo, price 5s.

ELEMENTARY SCHOOL ATLAS,
BY
A. KEITH JOHNSTON, LL.D.
FOR THE USE OF JUNIOR CLASSES.
Including a Map of Canaan and Palestine, and a General Index.

CONTENTS.

Map	Map
1 The World in Hemispheres, with Tables of the Heights of Mountains and Lengths of Rivers.	10 Spain and Portugal.
2 Europe.	11 Ottoman Empire in Europe and Asia, and Greece.
3 England and Wales.	12 Sweden and Norway.
4 Scotland and Ireland.	13 Russia and Poland.
5 France (in Provinces and Departments) and Switzerland.	14 Asia.
6 Belgium, Netherlands, and Denmark.	15 India—Australia.
7 Empire of Germany.	16 Africa and Arabia.
8 Austro-Hungarian Monarchy.	17 North and South America.
9 Italy.	18 United States and Canada.
	19 Central America and West India Islands.
	20 Canaan and Palestine.

TWELVE BLANK PROJECTIONS,

Corresponding in Scale with the Plates of KEITH JOHNSTON's General Atlas— viz., Europe, Asia, Africa, North America, South America, England, Scotland, Ireland, France, Spain, Italy, and Palestine. Price 2s. 6d. Single Projections, 3d. each.

TOURISTS' MAPS,
(SELECTED FROM THE 'ROYAL ATLAS.')
Mounted on Canvas, and bound in a Pocket-case.

				s.	d.
America (U.S.),	2 Sheets, with Index of	5675 Names,		8	0
America (South),	2 do.	„ 5400	„	8	0
Australia,	1 do.	„ 1980	„	4	6
Austria,	2 do.	„ 6300	„	8	0
Belgium and the Netherlands,	1 do.	„ 5300	„	4	6
Canada,	2 do.	„ 3070	„	8	0
China and Japan,	1 do.	„ 2420	„	4	6
England,	2 do.	„ 11,700	„	8	0
India,	2 do.	„ 7500	„	8	0
Ireland,	1 do.	„ 5270	„	4	6
Italy,	2 do.	„ 6170	„	8	0
Mediterranean Shores,	1 do.	„ 2170	„	4	6
Palestine,	1 do.	„ 3100	„	4	6
Prussia,	1 do.	„ 2550	„	4	6
Scotland,	2 do.	„ 9000	„	7	6
Spain and Portugal,	1 do.	„ 4100	„	4	6
Sweden and Norway,	1 do.	„ 1630	„	4	6
Switzerland,	1 do.	„ 4907	„	4	6

All the Maps in the 'Royal Atlas' may be had in separate sheets, price, with Index, 3s. per sheet.

PLANS OF LONDON.

		s.	d.
Collins' Map of London, with reference to Streets, in Case,		1	0
„ Coloured,		1	6
„ On Cloth, in Case,		3	6
Stanford's 12 Miles round London, in Case,		2	6
„ Coloured, on Cloth, in Case,		5	6
Map of the Environs of London, Plain, in Case,		1	0
„ „ Coloured,		1	6
„ „ „ and Mounted in Case,		3	0

LIBRARY AND OFFICE MAPS.

CHART OF THE WORLD

On Mercator's Projection (Johnston's) - Size, 72 by 56 inches. Price, in 4 Sheets, coloured, £1. 15s. 0d. ; on Mahogany Rollers, varnished, or in the Mercator Case, £3. 3s. ; Mounted on Frame, with Gilt Bead, varnished, £4. 10s. (For detailed description of this Map, see page 50.)

Maps of the Great Divisions of the Globe.

EUROPE,

Stanford's, constructed by A. Keith Johnston, LL.D., F.R.S.E., F.R.G.S., &c., Geographer to the Queen.—Size, 65 by 58 inches. Scale, 56 miles to 1 inch. Price, in 4 Sheets, coloured, £3. 3s. ; on Mahogany Rollers, varnished, £4.

Johnston's, constructed by A. Keith Johnston, LL.D.—Size, 44 by 41 inches. New and revised edition, price, in 4 Sheets, coloured, 15s. ; on Mahogany Rollers, varnished, 30s. (For detailed description of this Map, see page 51.)

ASIA,

Stanford's, constructed by A. Keith Johnston, LL.D. Size, 65 by 58 inches. Scale, 110 miles to 1 inch. Price, in 4 Sheets, coloured, £2. 2s. ; on Mahogany Rollers, varnished, £3.

Arrowsmith's — Size, 72 by 64 inches. Scale, 70 miles to 1 inch. Price, in 4 Sheets, coloured, £3. 3s. ; on Mahogany Rollers, varnished, £3. 3s.

INDIA,

Walker's, with the Telegraphs and Railways, from Government Surveys. Size, 60 by 65 inches. Price, in 4 Sheets, £2 ; in a Case, £3. 13s. 6d. ; on Rollers, varnished, £3. 3s.

AFRICA,

Stanford's, constructed by A. Keith Johnston, LL.D. - Size 65 by 64 inches. Scale, 76 miles to 1 inch. Price, in 4 Sheets, coloured, £3. 3s. ; on Mahogany Rollers, varnished, £4.

Arrowsmith's — Size, 76 by 64 inches. Scale, 65 miles to 1 inch. Price, in 4 Sheets, coloured, £3. 3s. ; on Mahogany Rollers, varnished, £3. 3s.

AMERICA, NORTH,

Stanford's, constructed by A. Keith Johnston LL.D.—Size, 62 by 58 inches. Price, in 4 Sheets, coloured, £3. 3s. ; on Mahogany Rollers, varnished, £3.

AMERICA, SOUTH,

Stanford's, constructed by A. Keith Johnston, LL.D.—Size, 65 by 58 inches. Price, in 4 Sheets, coloured, £3. 3s. ; on Mahogany Rollers, varnished, £3.

Arrowsmith's - Size, 90 by 80 inches. Scale, 45 miles to 1 inch. Price, in 6 Sheets, coloured, £4. 4s. ; on Mahogany Rollers, varnished, £7. 7s.

AMERICA, UNITED STATES OF,

Stanford's, constructed by A. Keith Johnston, LL.D.—Size, 75 by 58 inches. Scale 55 miles to 1 inch. Price, in 4 Sheets, coloured, £3. 3s. ; on Mahogany Rollers, varnished, £4.

AMERICA, NORTH AND SOUTH,

Arrowsmith's —Size, 78 by 64 inches. Scale 65 miles to 1 inch. Price, in 4 Sheets, coloured, £3. 3s. ; on Mahogany Rollers, varnished, £3. 3s.

AUSTRALASIA,

Stanford's, constructed by A. Keith Johnston, LL.D.—Size, 62 by 64 inches. Scale, 64 miles to 1 inch. Price, in 4 Sheets, coloured, £3. 3s. ; on Mahogany Rollers, varnished, £4.

TASMANIA,

By James Sprent, Surveyor-General.—Size, 46 by 44 inches. Scale 3 miles to 1 inch. Price, in 4 Sheets, coloured, £1, 14s. 6d. ; on Mahogany Rollers, varnished, £2, 12s. 6d.

BRITISH ISLES,

Smith's.—Size, 74 by 72 inches. Price, in 6 Sheets, coloured, £1, 10s. ; on Mahogany Rollers, varnished, £2, 12s. 6d.

Johnston's.—Size, 54 by 40 inches. Price, in 4 Sheets, 12s. ; on Rollers, varnished. (For detailed description of this Map, see page 46.)

ENGLAND,

Stanford's (from the Ordnance Triangulation). Size, 84 by 72 inches. Scale, 4 miles to 1 inch. Price, in 9 Sheets, coloured, £2, 12s. 6d. ; on Mahogany Rollers, varnished, £4, 4s.

Arrowsmith's.—Size, 54 by 60 inches. Price, in 4 Sheets, coloured, £4, 10s. 6d. ; on Mahogany Rollers, varnished, £5, 5s.

SCOTLAND,

Arrowsmith's.—Size, 54 by 60 inches. Price, in 4 Sheets, coloured, £2, 12s. 6d. ; on Mahogany Rollers, varnished, £3, 3s.

Ainslie's.—Size, 73 by 65 inches. Price, in 9 Sheets, coloured, £2, 2s. ; on Mahogany Rollers, varnished, £3, 3s.

Stanford's.—Size, 54 by 54 inches. Price, in Sheets, coloured, £2, 2s. ; on Mahogany Rollers, varnished, £3, 13s. 6d.

IRELAND,

Arrowsmith's.—Size, 54 by 60 inches. Price, in 4 Sheets, coloured, £2, 12s. 6d. ; on Mahogany Rollers, varnished, £3, 3s.

Railway Commissioners.—Size, 54 by 60 inches. Scale, 4 miles to 1 inch. Price, in 6 Sheets, coloured, £1, 14s. 6d. ; on Mahogany Rollers, varnished, £2, 2s.

LONDON,

Stanford's Library Map of.—Size, 59 by 50 inches. Scale, 6 inches to 1 mile. Price, in 16 Sheets, in Portfolio, plain, 25s. ; or coloured, 31s. 6d. ; on Mahogany Rollers, varnished, or in Morocco Case, 42s. 10s.

CENTRAL AND SOUTH-WESTERN EUROPE,

Extending from Denmark on the N. to Italy on the S., and from the Danube on the E. to Portugal on the W.—The new Historical Europe ; showing the New Boundaries of the European Empire, including Alsace and Lorraine, with Fortifications, Sites of Battles, and Railways, accompanied by a Descriptive and Historical Handbook. By A. Keith Johnston, LL.D., Geographer to the Queen. Size, 44 by 44 inches. Price on Rollers, varnished, 10s.

For Illustrations of the Various Modes of Mounting above Maps on Spring Rollers, etc., see page 40.

GEOLOGICAL MAPS.

GEOLOGICAL MAP OF THE BRITISH ISLES, Ramsay.—Size, 44 by 34 inches. Scale, 12 miles to 1 inch. Price, in 4 Sheets, coloured, £2, 12s. ; on Mahogany Rollers, varnished, £3, 3s.

GEOLOGICAL MAP OF ENGLAND AND WALES. By Andrew Ramsay, F.R.S., F.G.S., etc.—Scale, 12 miles to 1 inch. Price, in 1 Sheet, coloured, £1, 5s. ; in Case, £1, 12s. ; on Rollers, £2, 12s.

GEOLOGICAL MAP OF ENGLAND AND WALES. By Sir R. I. Murchison, D.C.L., etc.—Scale, 30 miles to 1 inch. Price, in 1 Sheet, coloured, 9s. ; in Case, 12s.

GEOLOGICAL MAP OF SCOTLAND. M'Culloch's.—Size, 54 by 60 inches. Price, in 4 Sheets, coloured, £4, ; on Mahogany Rollers, varnished, £5, 14s. 6d.

GEOLOGICAL MAP OF SCOTLAND, with Explanatory Notes. By Sir R. Impey Murchison, D.C.L., etc., and Archibald Geikie, F.R.S., F.G.S., etc., the Topography by A. Keith Johnston, LL.D., F.R.S.E., etc.—Size, 37 by 34 inches. Price, in Portfolio, etc.

GEOLOGICAL MAP OF IRELAND (Railway Commissioners' Map). Size, 54 by 60 inches. Scale, 4 miles to 1 inch. Price, in 6 Sheets, coloured, £3, 13s. 6d. ; on Mahogany Rollers, varnished, £5, 5s.

GEOLOGICAL MAP OF THE BRITISH ISLANDS. By Archibald Geikie, Esq., F.R.S., F.G.S., Professor of Geology in the University of Edinburgh. Price (with Hand-book) on Rollers, plain, £1, 1s. ; varnished, £1, 5s. ; folded 10s. in Portfolio, £1, 1s. ; folded free, in Case, £1, 6s. Size, 4 feet 3 inches by 3 feet 2 inches.

GEOLOGY OF EDINBURGH AND NEIGHBOURHOOD. By Professor Geikie. Price, Cloth, 1s. 6d.

JUST PUBLISHED,

HENRY F. BRION'S
SERIES OF RELIEVO MAPS.

Equally adapted for Schools, Libraries and Families ; constructed from the Works of Celebrated Geographers.

LIBRARY AND SCHOOL EDITION.

Size 22 by 18 inches, Framed in Rosewood and Gilt, 12s. 6d. ; Beaded Frames, 10s. 6d.

COLOURED POLITICALLY OR PLUVIALLY.

ENGLAND & WALES, SCOTLAND, EUROPE, PALESTINE, Ancient or Modern,
(with Vignette of Jerusalem.)

MINIATURE EDITION.

Size 8 by 7 in. ; Framed in Rosewood and Gilt, 2s. 6d. ; Beaded Frames, 2s. ; Unframed 1s. 3d.

ENGLAND & WALES Coloured Politically.
SCOTLAND   ,,   ,,
EUROPE   ,,   ,,
PALESTINE (with Vignette of Jerusalem).

Size 15 by 9½ inches ; Framed in Rosewood and Gilt, 6s. 6d. ; Beaded Frames, 5s. 6d.

ISLE OF WIGHT, reduced from the Geological Survey of England, by H. W. Bristow, F.R.S., F.G.S.

Other Maps are in the course of construction.

OPINIONS OF THE PRESS.

Illustrated London News.—"The engraving is in the best style of art. The surface is embossed in exact imitation of the undulations of the country, and are palpable to the eye in a way which no flat surface can possibly realise. The result is in every respect highly satisfactory."

Illustrated News of the World.—"The hills are carefully modelled. The whole map is very striking, and will convey at one glance more accurate ideas than could be acquired by years spent in mere abstract descriptions."

The Guardian.—"Pretty, and wonderfully cheap. More can be learned from these relievo maps in an hour than from ordinary maps in a week."

The Record.—"The most perfect production of the kind we have yet seen. Executed with beauty and precision."

OPINIONS FROM HER MAJESTY'S INSPECTORS OF SCHOOLS.

"Such maps are much wanted in all Schools."—"Your idea is a very good one, and I think it deserving of every encouragement."—"I have lately seen the maps in the exhibition at Munich, but there was nothing so exactly what is wanting in this Country, nor anything approaching the lowness of your price."—"I have seen nothing in England or on the Continent, which is more deserving of being encouraged in the Geographical line."

DICTIONARY OF GEOGRAPHY.

Descriptive, Physical, Statistical, Historical,

FORMING A COMPLETE GENERAL

GAZETTEER OF THE WORLD.

By A. KEITH JOHNSTON, LL.D., F.R.S.E., F.G.S., etc.

Price, full bound, cloth, 36s.

Extract from Preface to the First Edition.

"This work is intended to supply what was generally felt to be a desideratum—a GEOGRAPHICAL DICTIONARY, embracing within a convenient space, and of easy reference, a much greater number of names than is usually found in similar books, even when extending to several volumes; arranged according to a uniform and methodical plan, and combining, with the utmost attainable accuracy, the most authentic information up to the present time. The Author was induced to engage in this arduous undertaking, from a persuasion that his previous studies would afford him facilities for its execution, such as few have enjoyed, and from his being possessed of an extensive and valuable collection of Books, Maps, and Notes, relating to every portion of the globe. He has endeavoured to render these materials available for the production of a Standard Book of General Geographical Reference, by compressing every article into the smallest space consistent with distinctness, by the adoption of a single method of abbreviation, and by classing under one entry many places of the same name. Books of this kind are often chargeable with great inaccuracy in their statements of the positions and bearings of places. This may, in part, be accounted for by the difficulty of ascertaining the proper value of foreign measurements; but it is owing chiefly in such works being mere copies of pre-existing and erroneous compilations. The only remedy for this serious defect was found to be a constant reference to the best maps. Accordingly, in this Work, for the first time it is believed, the plan has been systematically followed of determining by measurement the position, extent, and bearing of every place described. No previously existing dictionary has been followed either in method or matter; every article has been written expressly for this work from original materials, and it will be found to contain many valuable notices from recent geographical and statistical works not otherwise accessible to the English reader."

Extract from Preface to the Edition of 1874.

"The eighth edition of the Dictionary of Geography has been subjected to a thorough revision during three years of continuous application, and the whole work has been reprinted in a manner which it is believed will much facilitate easy reference, since each leading name now appears in a bolder type than the descriptive text which follows it.

"Though the work has lost the invaluable supervision of its author, the true geographical spirit in which he would have carried out the new edition has been carefully kept in view; and no labour has been spared to procure from all quarters the best materials, in census tables and trustworthy information of all kinds, and to incorporate these in the Gazetteer. The tables of area and population throughout the Dictionary have been entirely recomposed, generally on the basis of the authentic statistics collected by Drs. Behm and Wagner of Gotha and published in the Gotha Almanac and the Geographical Year-Books. A new feature in the Gazetteer is the collection of the rest of the volume of all the tables, scattered throughout its pages, into one comparative series of the greater and lesser geographical and political divisions of the whole globe."

The Times (leading article).

"The best and most authoritative English Gazetteer now extant."

Companion to the Royal Atlas.

In One Volume, Imperial 8vo, pp. 680, price 21s.

INDEX GEOGRAPHICUS:

BEING A LIST, ALPHABETICALLY ARRANGED, OF THE

PRINCIPAL PLACES ON THE GLOBE,

WITH THE COUNTRIES AND SUBDIVISIONS OF THE COUNTRIES IN WHICH THEY ARE SITUATED,

AND THEIR LATITUDES AND LONGITUDES.

COMPILED SPECIALLY WITH REFERENCE TO

KEITH JOHNSTON'S ROYAL ATLAS,

AND APPLICABLE TO ALL MODERN ATLASES AND MAPS.

OPINIONS.

Spectator.

"It is in fact a gazetteer of unparalleled fulness. It must contain at least 63,000 names [147,000], of which it tells us the province and country in which they are situated, and their latitude and longitude, besides the reference to the Royal Atlas. What is the value of the rest of the information in half the gazetteers?"

Reader.

"To a certain extent, this thick and closely-printed royal octavo volume of 676 pages, in double columns, forms a condensed gazetteer of all the principal places on the globe, giving, besides their latitude and longitude, the exact subdivision of the country preceding the name of the country itself. . . . The entire volume exhibits some 150,000 names, in strict alphabetical order, and, as far as we have tested the book, giving such information as we have instanced above with extreme accuracy, and including, as well as those of the principal places, many names of such as are insignificant, and particularly those of towns in the colonies, America, India, and the East, and of places mentioned by African travellers. . . . Indeed we cannot but express the great satisfaction the work has given us, from the very comprehensive plan of its execution, in every instance in which we have consulted its pages, and we therefore have no hesitation in recommending it as one of the most useful books of ready reference to the geographical student, or as a valuable handbook for either the library or counting-house. . . . By far the most complete list of the names of places in existence."

Belfast News-Letter.

"It has seldom fallen to our lot to direct public attention to a more valuable and practically useful work than the above. In a royal octavo volume of nearly seven hundred pages we have a strictly alphabetical index to every recorded locality on the globe. Closely printed in double columns, each page contains nearly two hundred names, giving the names of the countries in which every place is situate, its latitude and longitude, the map where it is to be found, and a column of special index letters which point out its exact situation. . . . It is an indispensable requisite in every merchant's office, as well as to every public institution."

Maps, Plans, and other Publications

OF THE

Ordnance and Geological Survey Departments.

W. & A. K. JOHNSTON,

GEOGRAPHERS AND ENGRAVERS TO THE QUEEN,

4 ST. ANDREW SQUARE, EDINBURGH,

Having been appointed by the Secretary of State for War, AGENTS in Scotland for the sale of the above publications, are now enabled to supply these important works to the Public and the Trade. They furnish to order all the new sheets as published, *reduce or enlarge portions of the Survey*, and reproduce them by Lithography, to any scale, as Plans of Estates or Law Plans.

Sheets of the Survey can be joined together so as to make a complete Estate Plan or Plan of a Farm, which can be coloured and mounted on cloth to order.

Areas of Estates or Farms computed; Tables of Contents constructed; and Scotch or other measures converted into Imperial Acres.

Tracings procured of those portions of the Country which are surveyed but not yet published, and every information given as to the State of the Survey. A list of all the Counties, Parishes, and Towns published, sent free by Post, price Sixpence.

By Command of Her Majesty Queen Victoria.

Facsimiles of the National Manuscripts of Scotland,

SELECTED UNDER THE DIRECTION OF

THE LORD CLERK REGISTER OF SCOTLAND;

WITH

TRANSLATIONS AND NOTES.

COMPLETE IN 3 VOLS.

PRICE, 21s. EACH, FOLIO, BOUND CLOTH.

Facsimiles of the National Manuscripts of England,

From William the Conqueror to Queen Anne,

SELECTED UNDER THE DIRECTION OF

THE MASTER OF THE ROLLS; ·

WITH

TRANSLATIONS AND NOTES.

COMPLETE IN 4 VOLS.

PRICE, 16s. EACH, FOLIO, BOUND CLOTH.

Detailed Lists of the National Manuscripts may be had on application.

ENGRAVING AND PRINTING

IN ALL THEIR BRANCHES,

Including Atlases, Plans, Views, Bank
Notes, and Commercial Work.

PHOTOLITHOGRAPHY.

Exact Facsimiles of Drawings, Deeds, Charters, or other
Documents produced by this Process.

Process, Sederunt, Letter, and Note Papers,
of the various qualities kept on hand.

Bank Cheques, Invoice, and Letter-Headings
Engraved and Printed.

BUSINESS AND ADDRESS DIES,

COATS OF ARMS, CRESTS, AND MONOGRAMS,

Designed, Cut in Steel and Stamped Plain, or
Embossed in Gold or Colours.

LITHOGRAPHIC
DRAWING, WRITING, AND PRINTING.

Plans of Estates, Law Plans, etc.

ENLARGED OR REDUCED.

ILLUSTRATIONS FOR WORKS OF SCIENCE,

Illuminated Printing and Printing in Colours,

CAREFULLY EXECUTED TO ORDER.

Maps, Plans, or Drawings, Mounted on Cloth, Roller, or Case.